I0598858

THE SORCERESS

The Amulet Saga
Volume Five

by

Avily Jerome

THE SORCERESS
Published by Dragontail Press
PO Box 54550
Phoenix, AZ, 85078

ISBN 978-1-7321879-5-5
Copyright © 2019 by Avily Jerome
Cover art concept by Sarah Collotta
Cover design by Kirk DouPonce, Dog Eared Design

Available in print from your local bookstore, online, or from the author at: www.avilyjerome.com

For more information on this book and the author visit: www.avilyjerome.com

All rights reserved. Non-commercial interests may reproduce portions of this book without the express written permission of the author, provided the text does not exceed 500 words. When reproducing text from this book, include the following credit line: *"The Amulet Saga, Volume Five: The Sorceress* **by Avily Jerome, published by Dragontail Press. For more information visit www.avilyjerome.com. Used by permission."**

Commercial interests: No part of this publication may be reproduced in any form, stored in a retrieval system, or transmitted in any form by any means—electronic, photocopy, recording, or otherwise—without prior written permission of the author, except as provided by the United States of America copyright law.

This is a work of fiction. Names, characters, and incidents are all products of the author's imagination or are used for fictional purposes. Any mentioned brand names, places, and trademarks remain the property of their respective owners, bear no association with the author or the publisher, and are used for fictional purposes only.

Brought to you by Avily Jerome
And by Dragontail Press, www.avilyjerome.com

Library of Congress Cataloging-in-Publication Data
Jerome, Avily
The Sorceress/Avily Jerome 1st ed.

Printed in the United States of America.

1

For my Wonder Women
Lindsay, Sarah, and Catherine
I thank my God upon every remembrance of you

Acknowledgments

Special thanks to my husband, who supports me financially and emotionally, and who allows me to pursue my passion.

Thanks also to my dad, whose continual support for my writing and my books blesses me beyond words.

Thanks to my mom, who taught me to read and instilled in me an endless love of the written word.

And, of course, thank you to my readers, the ones who are still interested in what's going on in Legerdemain.

Table of Contents

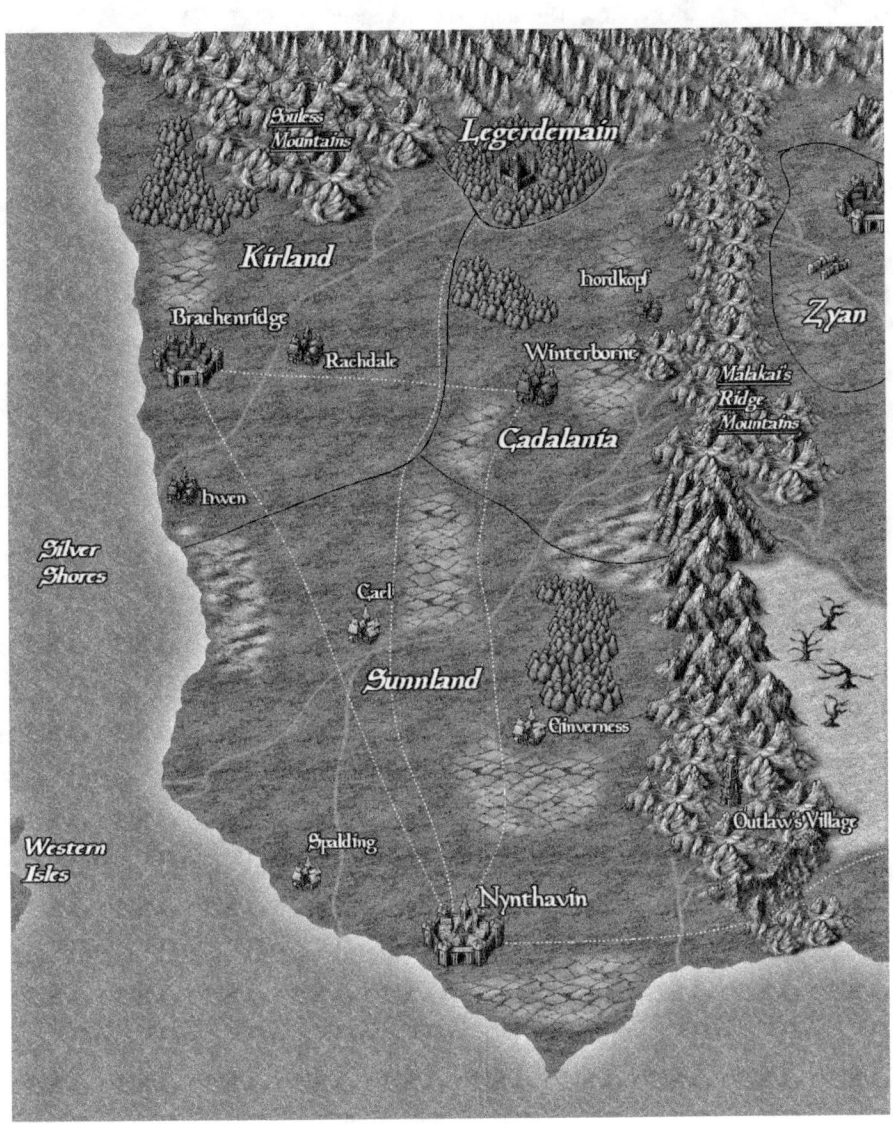

The daughter of the dragon
Who oversees the land
Will live until the day
The dragons come again

Love she'll never know
A child she'll never have
The kings and queens of fate
Her legacy will show

From the path fate strays
The Lover and the Traitor
When the Solstice Moon shines brightly
And at the Dragon, the Dancer waves

Across the ocean wide
The darkness rises swiftly
Untold power unleashed
Building until that day

The reign of power shifts
Fate in the balance
The weight of choices made
Brings life or the end of all

The child lost arises
To take the power back
A child of the enemy
Begotten then to conquer

When the dragons rise again
When the mountains open wide
When the stones of heaven fall
The world is remade.

When the darkness reigns
Then the hate shall bind
The hearts of one and all
Until the light is found

Those who triumph fall
Those who seek shall find
Those who rule shall serve
The servant, ruler of all

The begotten of the dragons
Beloved of the Creator
Who bears the Dragon Stone
The Deliverer of the World

THE SORCERESS

The Amulet Saga
Volume Five

Attacked

"They're coming," the watchman shouted.

Sir Cornan mounted his horse and drew his sword, filing into formation with the other soldiers. The gate opened and they rode out to meet the attacking army.

Just before the city gate slammed closed behind them, a young woman slipped through.

What was she doing? She was going to get herself killed. Cornan broke away and rode back toward her. "You shouldn't be out here. Get back before the battle starts."

She smiled, but her blue eyes held a hint of sadness. "It's too late. The king's orders are not to open the gate once it has been closed. Don't worry about me. I'm here to help you."

She reached out and placed one hand on his sword and the other on his horse. A pale glow spread through his sword and he felt a slight tingle as the glow washed over him. His horse pranced, seeming more energetic than he had a moment before.

"You should get back in formation. They're coming." The young woman walked down the line, touching each man and his horse. As soon as she finished, the captain gave the order to ride.

They passed through the South Village to where the enemy spread out on the plain beyond. Cornan joined his fellow soldiers. He hoped the woman would stay close to the castle, far away from the battle, but she swung up on the king's horse behind him.

The column thundered down the road, toward the empty village, and formed up facing the enemy.

Cornan took his place, but his eyes darted back toward the woman.

She dismounted from the king's horse. She'd be trampled! He was torn between his duty to hold the line and his desire to rescue the woman.

Then she spoke. Her voice carried above the sounds of men and horses. "Men of Ryshael, we have no wish to be at war with you. We can live peacefully as neighbors, but be warned, this is your last opportunity for truce. If you choose war, it will not end until you are annihilated."

The leader of the enemy army laughed. Despite his deep, booming voice, he was harder to hear than the woman. "On the contrary, my Lady, if you surrender now, the king will show mercy and allow your people to live as his subjects. He means to claim this land. How he takes it, by force or by peace, is up to you."

The woman nodded. "Then let it begin."

The enemy captain charged, his army following.

Cornan turned from watching the woman and charged into the battle. His first stroke sliced cleanly through his opponent. The tingling sensation the woman had touched him with ran through his arms, and despite how many times he struck, he did not seem to tire. All around him, his fellows were fighting with the strength of ten men, quickly pushing the enemy back.

Lightning flashed, though the sky was clear. In a matter of moments, the enemy was all but vanquished.

The Ryshaelan captain sounded the retreat and the enemy—those few who still lived—thundered over the plain and disappeared into the hills far to the south.

The woman stared after them, waiting until the last one disappeared from sight before climbing back up behind the king on his horse and directing him back toward the city.

Who was this woman, that the king himself deferred to her?

The king thundered back toward the castle and led the heads of divisions, including Cornan, into the Council room.

The woman took a seat at the king's right hand.

The king looked at her. "What do you think? Will they be back?"

"Most assuredly. This was just a small test of strength to determine how easy it will be to conquer us. Now they know we will not go down without a fight, they will most likely try to overwhelm us. They won't be able to tear us down a little at a time, which is what they were learning today, so they will bring their full forces against us."

"How long?"

"Two, three days. A week at the most."

"What do you suggest?"

"Harvest as many crops as possible and prepare the people for the eventuality that we will need to bring all the villagers and farmers into the city. The enemy will burn everything and then lay siege to the city. I'll do what I can to minimize the damage, but most of my strength will be needed for the battle."

The king nodded to a page. "Send out orders to begin harvesting and bring all the food to the palace storehouses immediately."

He turned back to the woman. "What else?"

"Every man of fighting age must be asked to fight. Their numbers are so far beyond ours, we'll be lucky to have one soldier to their ten. Also, there's one more, slight problem."

"What is it?" the king asked.

"They know about me now, so we can't rule out the possibility that they will enlist the help of a sorcerer as well. I'll have the advantage, since this is my land, but I won't be able to stop another sorcerer from accessing magic."

"Will they succeed?"

The woman smiled sadly. "You know I can't See that clearly. The future is too clouded. I do know we at least stand a chance."

The king kissed her lightly on the cheek. "Thank you, Ada."

She bowed and left the room.

Ada. Why did that name seem so familiar? Cornan sorted through his memories to pull up any association. Wasn't that the name of the midwife? He'd always imagined her to be a fat, middle-aged woman, not a beautiful maiden. And why hadn't he known that the palace midwife was also a sorceress? A powerful one, at that, if what he'd seen today was any indication.

The king touched a jewel that hung around his neck—an amethyst, set in an ornate gold setting.

"What do you want us to do?" the captain of the guard asked.

"You heard her," the king said. "Start preparing the villages and farms for the probability that they'll need to evacuate. Then, start recruiting. We'll need everyone who is able to join the fight. Better yet, create an envoy. I'll go speak to the people myself."

Merchant

"You understand what you're supposed to do?" the Jando, the Ryshaelan king asked.

The spy nodded. "Of course."

"And you think you're up to the task?"

The spy curled her lip in a sneer. "I was chosen for a reason. I am utterly unremarkable in every way. I am never noticed in a crowd, and I'm much too plain and uninteresting to be looked at twice. Don't think I don't know this. Yes, I know what to do and how to do it. I'll be back in three days with my report."

The king nodded. "Very well. Griston will meet you by the oak on the other side of the river at midnight. Don't fail me."

"I won't," the spy said.

She threw a cloak around her shoulders and, under the cover of darkness, made her way across the river and into Legerdemain. These people were far too trusting. She'd discovered that on her first scouting trip. All friendly and willing to help, never even considering that there might be ulterior motives.

On that trip, she'd heard that a merchant in the South Village had just lost his previous assistant to marriage and was looking for someone to take her place. It was the perfect position from which to garner information.

She skirted the South Village and spent the rest of the night in an old, unused barn a few miles north. When morning came, she dusted off her cloak and made her way into the village, just as the women were coming out to get water from the well in the square at the center of town.

They smiled and waved, in their open, friendly manner.

One woman, a sturdy, graying woman in her middle years, paused to beckon her.

The spy smiled shyly as she approached.

"G'day to ye, lass. Where ye be coming from?"

"The... the North Village," she said. "I heard from my cousin in the East village that she heard from her friend who is courting someone who is friends with someone who lives here that a merchant who lives here might be looking for help."

"Aye, right you are! That'll be Mago. Now, just follow this road here down past the house with the new thatch on the right, and turn left at that little street. If you see the blacksmith shop, you've gone too far. Mago's house has two stories, with a large storage barn out the back, and green shutters on all the windows. You can't miss it."

The spy smiled. "Thank you kindly, ma'am."

"My pleasure, Lass. I hope to be seeing more of you, if you stay." The woman went back to her bucket at the well, and the spy continued down the road. She'd already scouted out where the merchant lived, but it would corroborate her story to follow the woman's directions. Maybe even get lost a time or two and ask a few more people for help.

She passed the house with the new thatch and kept walking toward the blacksmith's shop.

The blacksmith stood in front of the forge, stoking the fire to prepare for the workday ahead.

"Mornin'," he called out to her.

The spy stood, as though uncertain, and then approached him. "I'm looking for the home of Mago the merchant. A woman at the well told me if I saw the blacksmith I've gone too far, but I'm not sure which way she said to go now."

"Ah, right you are. Just back that way, you see the house with the flowers along the path? Turn right back there, and go to the end of the street."

She made her way at last to the merchant's door and knocked.

Her words tumbled out in a rush when he opened the door, the same story she'd told the woman in the square.

Mago eyed her. "It's true, I am looking for a new assistant. But I need someone who is up for carrying heavy boxes and working hard."

"I'm stronger than I look, and I'm willing to learn," she said eagerly.

"Well..." he hesitated just long enough to pretend he was still considering it, even though she could see in his eyes he'd already decided to hire her.

"I s'pose we could give it a try. See how it goes for a week or two before we decide for sure."

She nodded. "Oh, thank you! You won't be disappointed."

"Well, come on in. You can put your things in the gable room—that was my old assistant's room—and I'll show you to the shop."

She shadowed him as he went to the market the next day, picking out which items from the local craftsmen he thought would sell well in the south and selling the things he'd imported on his last trip abroad.

The work itself was easy enough, and the benefits were tremendous. Gossip in the marketplace was rampant. The air was filled with speculation about the possibility of war. But most of the people were convinced that the king's sorceress had driven off the invaders for good. No one could stand up to magic. The battle had proved that.

The king himself was planning a visit to the Four Villages—in just a few days he'd come to tell them all the good news, that the invaders had been driven off and all was well.

The spy smiled to herself. One skirmish, and they thought they were invulnerable.

This war would be so easy. Very, very soon, this fertile land would belong to Ryshael.

On the appointed night, she crept out of Mago's house and took a horse from his stable, riding as fast as the horse could manage, all the way to the lone oak that stood by the river.

Her contact waited, as promised.

She told him all the news, including that the king was expected to visit and make an announcement.

When her contact left, she leaned against the tree, breathing deeply. She had to get back before anyone in Mago's household awoke, but both she and the horse needed a few moments to rest. Her hand brushed the rough bark. Despite the chill of the late winter air, her hand warmed. The tree felt familiar somehow, almost like a friend.

She drew her hand away quickly. The whole country was accursed with strange magic. The sooner Ryshael overtook it, the better.

Evacuation

"The king is coming!"

News of his arrival began buzzing the moment the scout arrived at the first farm south of the city. The farmer packed up his wife and children and hurried down to the South Village to hear what news the king would bring.

The spy and Mago heard about it from a fur trader who had delayed his hunting trip to the foothills in order to hear what the king had to say.

"He'll be here within the hour," the trader said. "Everyone is congregating in the square."

"I s'pose that means us, too," Mago sighed. "I hope this doesn't delay my next trip. I was hoping to get some of the early spring wine from Cadalania before the spring festivals."

The spy smiled sympathetically. "I'm sure it will be fine."

He nodded. "Come on, then. We'd better get down there."

The spy followed him, still with her demeanor of submission and timidity firmly enshrouding her.

The townspeople smiled and greeted her, making small talk and asking how she was settling in. She answered in positive, generic sentences, smiling timidly and expressing her gratefulness to have found such a good job.

True to the rumors, the king's entourage arrived shortly after she and Mago had found places to stand among the others.

She glanced around, looking for anyone who might be Ryshaelan, but she couldn't tell for sure. So many faces in this village were still unfamiliar to her, and there was no distinctive Legerdemainian facial feature, so she couldn't tell who was foreign and who was local.

The nation had been founded by refugees from all over the continent after the Great War, so there were hints of every race, from the white-haired, broad-shouldered barbarians from across the channel to the south, to the swarthy, pointed noses and almond-shaped eyes of Oajurans who were all but wiped out on the rest of the continent, to the pale skin and dark eyes of the Kirish people, to the dark-skinned Sunnlanders and brown-toned Cadalanians, and every possible combination therein amongst the people in the square.

It worked in her favor, since none of the locals immediately recognized her olive skin and tilted eyes as Ryshaelan, but it made it hard to spot an ally.

The king dismounted from his horse and stood upon the dais.

The spy was surprised to see how handsome he was. She didn't know what she'd expected—older and harder, like her own king, perhaps. But certainly not the soft, kind brown eyes that gazed affectionately at his people or the easy smile that graced his lips or the strand of hair that fell over his forehead, giving him a certain boyish charm.

"My people," he said, his voice deep and rich and full of empathy. "I come bearing dire news. Our scouts inform us that the Ryshaelan army, though it has retreated from our borders somewhat, has not returned home. War is upon us."

The spy bit her lip. This was not good news. The rumors that the townspeople had spread about the war being over were now proved false, which meant Ryshael had lost the element of surprise.

"We will try our utmost to preserve your homes and farms, but when they invade—and we are quite certain they will invade—the South Village will be the first to be overrun. I am very sorry to have to inform you of this, but you must prepare your things immediately, and be ready to evacuate as soon as word is given."

A murmur of protest rose up, but the king silenced it by raising his hand. "Quarters are being prepared in the city, so you will have a place to stay until the war is over. But I'm afraid this is not the extent of the dire news I have for you."

Silence reigned as the people waited to hear how much worse it could be.

"Our army is outnumbered, at least ten to one. There is no way we can defeat the Ryshaelans. We need every able-bodied man to enlist immediately. We need every blacksmith working on weapons, every farmer storing food and helping to prepare. Every single Legerdemanian is needed for this war effort."

A moan rose up.

One man—the tavern keeper, she thought—stepped forward. "All due respect, Majesty, but… why? If it's hopeless, why bother risking our lives and our families and our livelihoods for this? Why not just surrender peacefully and keep on living as we have been, but under Ryshaelan rule instead of yours?"

The spy perked up. Her king would want to hear if this idea took hold.

The king looked at the man for a long time before answering. "If I thought we could surrender peacefully and I could spare the lives of my people, I would do so."

The spy made a note to inform her king of this development. If they could take the country without bloodshed…

"Unfortunately, I have no reason to believe that to be the case. Have you ever heard of a people called the Vunderym?"

Around the square, people shook their heads.

The name sounded familiar to the spy… why? Where had she heard it before?

"They were a small nation, nestled between Cadalania and Sunnland, just east of Ryshael," the king said. "They'd established a small, peaceful country, comprised mainly of farms, after the Great War. It was one of the few pockets left on the continent where magic use was still accepted. Ryshael views magic as a taint, an unholy and unnatural defect. And they view themselves as superior. The only race worthy of existence. They wiped out the Vunderym, completely annihilating anyone who used magic, and anyone who opposed them. The children and the weak were enslaved, and every trace of their culture was erased, so no one who has not studied history knows they ever existed."

The king swept his gaze over the crowd before returning it to the man who had spoken. "They will do the same here. They will kill or enslave us, destroy our monuments, burn our histories and maps. They will take our land and mine the mountains, and in a generation, it will be as though Legerdemain had never existed."

The man who had objected squared his shoulders. "Well, then. I reckon I'll be signing up for the army."

That evening, Mago sat down at his table across from the spy. "I've been thinking. I'm going to sign up for the army. You've hardly been with me long enough to train, and I apologize for that, but I'm going to have to close the shop until after the war. If we lose, well, I guess it won't matter much, but if we win, then I'll need an apprentice again. I'll pay your wages, and a little extra so you have something to live on until you find more work."

The spy nodded. "Thank you. I… I suppose I'll board at the tavern for now. Thank you for allowing me to work this long."

"There's a good girl. Pray the Creator that we win this war quickly."

That night, the spy waited until she heard Mago snoring, then took a horse and rode for the river.

Rivers

Ada examined the map on the table in the king's study, the room adjacent to the throne room. The cartographers had improved upon the maps of the previous generation, charting the flow of the river more precisely and giving the mountains more detail.

She held back a sigh at the sight of the mountains. One day, she could return there. But that day was yet a long way off.

Longer than she cared to think about.

The natural bend of the Sapphire River as it wound around the edge of the valley before turning west toward the ocean made a perfect natural boundary, but it was too slow and shallow to provide much protection. The bridge along the South Road, built for trade, could be blocked, but there were too many other areas that could be forded.

"Good afternoon, Ada."

She glanced up at the King. "Hello, Ondrei."

"What are you working on?" he asked.

"I'm trying to figure out a way to improve our defense system," she said. "We're in an unprotected valley. There are simply too many fronts to manage if Ryshael decides to launch a full-on invasion. Farms, homes—not to mention the Villages—will all be destroyed. We need a way to keep an invading force out while still allowing for a reasonable trade route."

Ondrei took a step closer so he could look over her shoulder. He pressed in so his body brushed hers, seemingly innocently, but a little too contrived to be believable as a mistake.

She stepped to the side, putting some space between them. He was growing bolder with his attentions. She'd have to say something, eventually. She hoped her gentle rebuffs would suffice, but she knew, deep down, that he wouldn't give up so easily.

"The Sapphire River runs along our southern border, here," she said, pointing to the map, and the Wyvern comes down this way. If we could redirect the Sapphire more west, and Wyvern east, just for a short space, we could surround the entire country by a border of water."

"Wouldn't that affect the farmland that the Wyvern feeds?" Ondrei asked.

Ada shook her head. "Most of that land is swampland, unusable for growing crops. Digging out a channel for the river would actually make that land more useable, because it would direct the water to one location instead of having tributaries going in every direction. If it's deep enough, it will be a deterrent to invasion from the west and at least part of the south."

"What of the trade routes?"

"We can take the South Road to where it branches just south of the Sapphire. Use that as our primary trade route. It will take longer to get to the coast, but only marginally, and the distance will be worth the increased security."

Ondrei took a step closer again, his arm brushing hers as he pointed to the wavy line demarking the Wyvern, and traced it along the outer border of Legerdemain.

"Along here?"

Ada stepped away again, this time moving to the other side of the table. "Yes," she said. "And the Sapphire—I think if we build a dam here, at the base of the mountain, we can control the flow of the river, making it flow more heavily at times when we want to discourage travel across it. There are also various tributaries up in the mountains along here, that, if we redirect into the lake that the dam will form, will help significantly improve the overall volume."

"You want men to go into the mountains?"

Ada took a deep breath. "I know it's dangerous." She'd helped plant those rumors, the ones that suggested anyone traveling the Soulless Mountains faced certain death. But she'd also sworn to protect this land, and at the moment that vow superseded her vow to keep the mountains safe from humans—and the other way around.

"We need them to channel all the water they can into the Sapphire, and build a dam that can be opened or closed at will to control the flow of water into the valley."

"That will take weeks. Months, perhaps. And we need all of our able-bodied men in the army."

"It won't take that long if we use magic."

Ondrei stared at her, eyes narrowing. They'd had this discussion, so many times she couldn't count them. She'd had the same argument with his father, and his father's mother. The idea that magic was too powerful to be trusted to the populace was so ingrained in humankind, that they refused to even acknowledge its uses. Only the very elite were trained to use it, and thus the ability to wield it had all but been lost.

Ada had been trying for generations to undo that kind of thinking. Ondrei's father had allowed her to train a select few who showed great ability to be Healers during the plague, but the mindset that kept the rest of the world in fear of magic use still permeated Legerdemain, as well.

"Ondrei took a deep breath. "I can't. If we allow it now, then there will be no stopping it. In time, magic users will take over everything and control everyone. We cannot allow a few people to have so much power."

"Then allow everyone to have so much power. If you allow magic to be used as a resource, like the soil of the earth or the water in the rivers, with everyone having equal access to learn and glean, then it won't become a danger. No one person can ever control it all if there's always a possibility of another being more powerful or more able."

Ondrei shook his head. "I hear what you're saying, but it's just too risky."

Ada stepped closer and glared up at him. "It's too risky not to. The Ryshaelans have ten times our numbers. Maybe more. We cannot win this war if we don't change the rules."

She put a hand on his arm. "Magic use was banned, not to protect the *people*, but to protect the *nobility*. They couldn't stand the thought that the populace might be able to fight back against tyranny, to protect themselves or make their own decisions. They could only have power if they could control the power of the people. The idea that they must be protected by the kings and rulers rather than protect themselves because they're too weak or stupid to be able to think for themselves is an antiquated notion. Your leadership is not lessened because your people are strong—it is increased."

Ondrei looked at the map.

"You don't think we can win?"

"I know we cannot."

"And you believe this plan—diverting the rivers and building the dam—will offer us protection?"

"I do. But only some. We still need magic users."

Ondrei exhaled, his shoulders slumping in defeat. "Very well. I will give the order to begin building the dam. You may…" he gulped, "you may start training people in magic use."

Gossip

"I need to see the king," the spy said.

Her contact spat. "The king is preparing for war. You talk to me."

"I have urgent news that I must give to him directly. Take me to him."

"He's too busy for you."

"Fine. I'll find him myself." She pushed past him and lowered herself into the little boat he'd used to cross the river to meet her.

"Hey! Wait!" her contact yelled.

She ignored him and began paddling. He splashed into the water behind her and grabbed hold of the boat, nearly capsizing it trying to climb in.

"This is not acceptable," he sputtered.

"You can take it up with my uncle when we get there."

She rowed to the opposite bank and mounted his horse, which stood picketed in the field, quietly munching grass.

"You coming?" she asked.

He clambered up behind her, still grumbling, and she sent the horse flying toward the Ryshael camp.

She paused at the patrol to identify herself, then rode on toward the center of the camp where her uncle's tent sat, and dismounted.

Her contact trailed behind her as she thrust open the flap, alerting the guards who stood just inside.

"Wake him up. I must speak to him immediately."

"It's the middle of the night," one of the guards protested.

"Yes, exactly, which is why I used the term 'wake.' Hurry up."

The guard pushed through the curtain to the other side. Sounds of low voices and the shuffling of feet wafted through, and a few moments later her uncle appeared.

"You'd better have a good reason for this," he grumbled.

"I do, Majesty. I came immediately as soon as I heard. The Legerdemainians know we're planning to attack again. The king himself visited the villages to call the men to war."

"Well, there goes the element of surprise," her uncle murmured, stroking his long beard. "Did he say what their strategy would be?"

"No. He did say that they were outnumbered."

"Any chance they'll surrender?"

"It seems unlikely," the spy said. "The king told the people they'd be slaughtered or enslaved. They plan to fight."

He shrugged. "Then they leave us no choice but to overwhelm them. Anything else?"

The spy paused. She wanted to ask, but she couldn't be sure how he'd react...

"Well, spit it out, girl. What?" the king asked.

"They have a sorceress."

"I know. She killed dozens of our men in the first skirmish. What of it?"

"Why don't we have one, to fight for our side?"

The king strode across the tent and slapped her across the face. "Such a thing is an affront to the gods. Such power is not to be used for personal gain. Anyone who uses magic risks annihilation by the gods for their hubris. We will not speak of such things, and we will destroy anyone who offends the gods with their sorcery. Is there anything else you want to know, or can I go back to bed?"

The spy swallowed her fear. "Just one more question. Who were the Vunderym?"

Her uncle's eyes narrowed. "Where did you hear that name?"

She shrugged. "Local town gossip. They fear us because of the Vunderym."

"As well they should. The Vunderym were a weak, pathetic people who claimed there were no gods, only one Creator, and that the gifts he gave were for all. We vanquished them for their heresy."

The spy nodded. "I'll be back with my next report two nights from now."

She turned and left the tent, nearly stumbling over her contact on the way out. "I'm borrowing your horse," she told him. "I'll leave him picketed by the river."

Before he could sputter a response, she was on the horse, galloping back toward Legerdemain.

By dawn, she was in her bed in Mago's house, and a few hours later, she stood on the steps of the tavern. The tavern keeper, a thin, sour-looking woman, opened the door. "I was wondering… do you perchance have any work?"

"Aren't you Mago's apprentice?"

She nodded. "Yes, but he is closing his shop to join the army. I…" she sniffed and wiped away an imaginary tear. "Please, I can't go home."

The tavern keeper's face softened. "Come on in. I'm sure I have something you can do."

She served tables that night, listening carefully for any news she could carry back across the river. Most of it was the usual gossip—those in favor of joining up and fighting the enemy, those who thought the threat wasn't as bad as they were saying and it was a fear-mongering tactic to get more taxes, and those who believed that a peaceful resolution could be reached if they could just talk about it. A few other voices chimed in, but those were the main ones.

Would peaceful resolution be possible? Her uncle had been so… vague. Would he allow Legeremain to surrender without bloodshed? Or was there truth to the story of the Vunderym?

Perhaps, if she told him there were those who would be willing to surrender, he would be able to send an emissary. Perhaps King Ondrei would see reason.

Her uncle did not like to be told what to do, but she would craft her report in such a way as to make him see the possibility as favorable.

The next day, she worked cleaning up the previous night's messes, scrubbing tables in between serving the handful of patrons that came and went during the day. Evening would be when the crowds gathered, but there were enough people yet to keep her busy.

The door to the tavern slammed open, sending a shaft of bright light into the room, silhouetting a young woman.

"Have you heard?" she panted. "Ada is recruiting people to learn sorcery!"

The spy choked back the bile that rose in her throat.

They were going to *teach* it? To *people*? Not just Healers and the king's chosen, but… regular people? How could they? How could they even think it?

"Ada is going around to the villages as we speak," the woman in the doorway said. "She's going to the West and North today, and then the East tomorrow, and in the afternoon, she'll be coming here. We're to gather in the square for testing, to see which of us is able to do magic!"

It could not be. It couldn't be allowed to happen. But maybe there would still be time to stop it. Legerdemain would eventually be conquered, but if they could be convinced to surrender, it would be best for everyone.

For the second time in a row, that night she insisted on making her report directly to the king.

"Majesty, I have news of great importance. I have been working in the tavern. There is great unrest in Legerdemain. I believe they can be convinced to surrender, and be gently absorbed into our culture. If you send an emissary, promise that they can join us without bloodshed or death, they will surrender."

"My dear, foolish girl," her uncle sneered. "You are so like your father. And this is exactly why I challenged him to combat and the crown was passed to me. There is no such thing as quiet submission. If you leave any room for doubt, you will inevitably have insurrections and rebellions. Sheer force is the only way to conquer. They must be taught who is in control."

The spy gulped. "In that case, you should be aware that they will not go down without a fight. Even now, the head sorceress is preparing to teach magic to commoners. She is recruiting any who have the ability and planning to teach them how to wield magic against us. She will be in the South Village tomorrow afternoon."

Testing

"I always knew I was special. Different," one woman said to the girl next to her.

"My mama always accused me of practicing sorcery," the girl replied with a hushed giggle. "I guess we'll see if she was right."

Ada fought to maintain her composure as she wound her way through the throng to the front of the town square in the North Village. The truth that these people had never been told was that most people could sense magic, and even use it to varying degrees, but few would have the discipline and fortitude to develop that ability to any sort of meaningful strength.

She stood on the stone dais and lifted her hand. Closing her eyes, she pulled on the magical energy in the air, drawing it into herself, and then channeling it out her fingertips. She formed a ball of light that spun and danced in the air above her, and let it go until it captured the attention of all those gathered before her.

When a hush fell and the last lingering chatterers had given her their attention, she opened her eyes and smiled. She drew the light ball back into her hand and closed her hand in a fist, giving the illusion that she had just snuffed it out.

"Welcome," she said, amplifying her voice to be heard across the square. "You have come because you wish to learn magic. As the king's proclamation declared, the kingdom is in need of your help. The threat from Ryshael grows greater by the day, and we need those who can wield the energy of the earth to protect ourselves."

She scanned the faces in the crowd, the eager and the terrified and all those in between. "Today, we will do a simple test to determine who has the ability to sense and control magical energy. Those of you who show promise will return with me to the city, where I will train you in the magical arts."

Murmurs rippled through the crowd.

"If using magic in war, for the defense of your country, is not a practice you would like to pursue, you may return to your homes. The king has no desire to force anyone to do anything they do not feel comfortable doing."

She waited a moment while a small handful of people edged away from the crowd and disappeared into the cobbled streets that led away from the square.

"Please close your eyes," she said.

Those who remained obeyed.

"Magic is all around us. It is as much a part of nature as the sun in the sky, the wind on your face, and the grass under your feet. You rely on the sun and the water to make your plants grow, but magic is equally a part of the process. Magic and nature feed off one another, and you can harness magic from the world around you and bend it to your will, much the same as you would capture water in a bucket to nourish your crops or build a home from the wood of a tree to provide a shelter from the elements."

She kept her voice low, a smooth cadence that, though they didn't know it, matched the rhythm of the magic pulsing through the air, and made them more receptive to sensing its power.

"Reach out with your mind," she said. "Feel in the sun and the wind and the grass until you find a sensation that feels like it's glowing."

That wasn't really what was happening, but it was the best way she could describe the sensation to someone who didn't know what magic felt like.

"When you find the glow, pull on it with your mind. Imagine it's a rope and you're winding it up. Draw it into you."

She could see the frustration on a few faces—those who didn't understand or didn't feel the glow. Others scrunched in deep effort—those who could just grasp it, but who were not in tune with the world around them, who had too many other thoughts going through them to truly concentrate and embrace the magic.

Most of the crowd had looks of concentration, biting their lips or furrowing their brows just a little. They could feel the magic, and were drawing on the glowing rope she'd described.

31

However, a very few wore expressions of peace, joy almost rapturous as they lifted their faces to the sky. Those were the people who had the strongest affinity for magic, who were in tune with the ebb and flow of energy as it swirled around them. Those were the people who would make the finest Healers… and also the most deadly warriors.

"When you have the rope coiled, imagine it into a candle. The rope is the wick. Hold it in front of you, and light it. When you have it lit, bring it to me."

Almost instantly, a smattering of lights popped into existence above people's hands. Small shouts of joy accompanied the discovery as those who had succeeded realized their success. Those who had accomplished creating a light made their way to Ada.

"Very good," she smiled at them. One by one, she told them, "You are under no obligation to fight in the war. You may come and learn magic, no matter what you decide later. If you would like to come, go wait with my guards." All those who had achieved immediate success followed her gesture and went to stand by the contingent of soldiers Ondrei had sent with her.

The soldier in charge caught her eye. He stared at her, intense fascination in his eyes. She'd seen that look before. Ondrei wore it almost constantly. But this soldier seemed different. It wasn't just desire or longing or admiration, it was… what was it?

That she couldn't quite define the expression both worried her and intrigued her.

She turned her attention back to her pupils. "Keep trying. It doesn't always come easily at first. Surrender yourself to the glow. Allow it to fill you. Then try to light your candle again."

A few more succeeded in creating a ball of light, while a few others gave up and wandered away.

"Magic has a rhythm, like music. Listen to the wind. Do you hear it? Do you hear the song of magic? Follow the sound with your heart, and draw it into your soul. Try again."

She glanced over at those who stood to the side. Most still held their magical lights, studying them, listening to the magic pulsating through it and analyzing the feel of the energy that flowed through them.

The soldier still stared at her. Who was he? She'd seen him on the battlefront, and in the War Council, but who was he?

"I must go," Ada told the remaining people in the square. "But continue practicing. If you find you can summon the light, you may come to the castle and show me, and you will be given a place with the magic learners."

She walked toward the soldiers and her pupils. The soldier smiled at her and helped her onto her horse. Why did she fascinate him so? And why did that look in his eyes send tingles through her that had nothing to do with the magic she had constantly flowing through her?

Assassin

Cornan watched as the woman led the people gathered around her through the exercises. He'd seen her do the same thing in the three other villages, beginning with the West, moving to the North, then the East, and now the South. The crowd here was larger than at any of the others, partly because the South Village was the largest village, and partly because the people here had had more notice before Ada came to their village.

Only a few soldiers remained with him. Most had taken the recruits from the East Village back to the palace to get settled in, and would meet them here that evening to escort the people back to the palace in the morning. He had volunteered to stay with the sorceress, as part of the bodyguard contingent.

Most of the others were happy to take turns transporting recruits back and forth—it was far more interesting than standing around all day watching a bunch of people meditating—but Cornan didn't want to leave the sorceress.

He considered joining in the exercises. Something tugged at him as he listened to Ada's calm, soothing voice instruct the people on how to feel the magic all around them, how to connect with it and let it flow through them, and how to bend it to their will. He could almost feel the light she described, and a part of him longed to embrace it.

But he had to do his duty first, and that meant keeping his eyes open, his wits alert.

Someone at the back of the crowd moved, his eyes no longer closed, but focused intently on Ada.

Cornan tensed as he watched the man take a step nearer to Ada.

Moving slowly, so as not to attract the man's attention, Cornan also moved closer, angling so he would be in position to intercept the man.

Step by step, the man and Cornan each crept toward the sorceress, who seemed totally unaware of anything beyond her smooth, musical words.

Something flashed in the man's hand.

Cornan narrowed his eyes. The man had drawn a knife. Taking the last few steps at a run, Cornan drew his sword and planted himself between the would-be assassin and Ada, sword pointing at the man's heart. "Drop it," he snarled.

The man choked. He'd been so intent on his target, he hadn't seen Cornan until he stood in the way. Very quickly, however, his expression of shock changed to one of derision. "Your witch will not be our downfall."

In one swift motion, he launched the knife directly toward Ada.

Cornan jumped toward it.

He was too late.

The knife flew past him.

He fell with a thud onto the cobbles. He rolled to his feet and turned—he would have to work fast to stop the bleeding and get her to a Healer—if she wasn't killed instantly.

But there was no blood.

The knife hovered in the air in front of Ada's chest, held by some invisible force.

Ada looked at it, almost curiously, before plucking it from the air and holding in in her hands. She looked at the assassin, who had staggered back, into the clutch of one of the other soldiers.

"Who sent you?" she asked.

"You'll get nothing from me," the assassin spat.

Ada's brilliant blue eyes filled with regret. "I wish you would cooperate. If you will not, I will have to turn you over to the king's interrogators. I will be forced to supply a potion that will encourage you to speak, and the interrogators will do what they must until they glean every word of knowledge you carry about your army and your king's intentions."

"I won't speak—not a word," the assassin snarled.

Ada nodded sadly. "Yes, you will." She looked at the soldier. "Shackle him."

She spoke a few words in a language Cornan didn't understand, and the assassin slumped, his eyes glazing over in a trance-like stupor.

She turned to Cornan. "You would've taken the knife for me."

Cornan bowed. "Of course, my lady. It is my duty. But I missed. I failed you. For that, I am sorry."

"You didn't fail me. You—" She smiled, cutting off whatever she had been planning to say. "I'm still alive."

She turned back to the people, who had grown restless during the confrontation with the assassin. "I apologize for the interruption. However, it was a beautiful example of the power that can be achieved when you can wield magic. Now, if you are ready to begin again, close your eyes. Breathe deeply."

She continued on with the exercises, and Cornan made his way to the other soldiers, who held the assassin captive.

"She's right, you know," he said. "You will talk."

"I'll die first," the assassin said, his speech still sluggish from whatever spell Ada had put on him.

"I understand why you are here," Cornan went on, ignoring his protests. "It was a good plan. The sorceress demolished an entire unit of your army—you won't stand a chance once she trains more like herself. Kill her, destroy Legerdemain. Better to do it quickly, rather than risk facing a whole army of sorcerers."

He shackled the man's feet and wrists, and tied him to the back of a horse, immobile.

"It's too late, though. There are already those who can use magic and who know its powers. You may think you'll escape somehow. Get another chance to complete your mission. But you won't. You'll tell us everything you know."

"If you're so sure," the assassin mumbled, "why are you so keen to intimidate me?"

"Because if you survive interrogation, we'll send you back to your people. And I want you to be able to tell them, first hand, just what they're up against if they attack."

"In the end, it won't matter" the assassin's voice slurred. "You may have your sorceress and her apprentices, but we have power you cannot imagine. Legerdemain will fall, and you will watch your beloved sorceress burn."

Cornan selected three of the soldiers to take the prisoner to the castle.

Ada selected her apprentices, and told them to meet her back in the plaza at dawn to go to the palace.

Cornan accompanied her to the inn. "My lady, I must again apologize for earlier. I cannot live with myself, knowing I would have let an assassin kill you. If you hadn't used magic…"

She held up a hand to silence him. "You didn't fail me. I didn't use magic to stop the knife. You did."

Recruit

The spy stared at the sorceress.

How… how was that possible? The assassin could not have missed. And yet the sorceress saved herself.

She whispered something to the soldier who had stepped in the way, but the spy couldn't hear what it was.

But perhaps this was enough to convince the sorceress to stop what she was doing. Perhaps this would show her that what she was doing was wrong…

The soldiers bound the assassin and tied him to a horse, and three of the guards led him in the direction of the castle. The spy hated to imagine what kinds of torture he was destined for. But perhaps she could finish the job. Her uncle would surely have some respect for her if she could accomplish what his trained assassin could not.

The sorceress smiled. "I'm terribly sorry for that interruption. Where were we? Oh yes, close your eyes. Feel the light."

The spy had to think, to figure out a way to get close to the sorceress. Perhaps if she pretended to be a student.

She closed her eyes, listening as the sorceress wove her spell over the others. The spell was powerful—the spy could almost feel the light the sorceress said was there, could almost feel the trees waving their limbs in the fields, the grass swaying gently, the pulsing energy that flowed through everything…

She snapped her eyes open. She would not be lured in by this trickery.

But what she saw made her want to choke again.

One by one, lights appeared throughout the crowd. How was the sorceress doing this? Making them believe they themselves had made those lights?

38

Or had they?

Could all these people, men and women, young and old—could *all* of them wield magic?

The thought sickened her.

But those who held a light aloft in their hands were invited to go stand with the soldiers, and to come to the castle to be trained.

In just a little while, the sorceress would leave, and the spy's chance would be gone.

She considered trying to just kill her, but she was not even trained. She would fare no better than the assassin, and then her king would have no one to bring him reports. She had to figure out a way to go with the others. Perhaps as a scullery maid in the castle kitchens… but she'd be far busier there than even at the tavern. She'd never be able to find out anything useful to report to her king, and she certainly would not have the opportunity to kill the sorceress.

No, she had to go with the sorceress. Become someone trusted.

Which meant she had to pass this test.

May the gods forgive her.

She closed her eyes and tried to remember the instructions the sorceress had given, about feeling the light, drawing it in, focusing it…

She could still feel the trees, down to their roots and even the acorns they dropped that had not yet sprouted. A rush of energy swept through her as she connected to the power that flowed through the air and plants.

She opened her eyes.

A light glowed in her palms.

She gasped. It was horrible… and yet it was wonderful. She'd never felt more alive. Never more vibrant. Never had her existence mattered like it did in that moment.

"Very good," the sorceress smiled at her. "Would you like to join the others?"

In a daze, the spy carried her light over to the wagon and stood next to the others who had succeeded.

There were dozens more already at the castle when they arrived late that evening.

The sorceress drew them all together in the courtyard outside the castle gates. "We will have our first real lesson in the morning," she said. "Tonight, I want to discuss a little about what magic is for, and what it does, and answer any questions you may have."

She waited to see if anyone would ask anything right away, then launched into her lecture. "Magic is a part of the world. It is a tool, neither good nor evil, but only what the user deems. Like any tool, it can be dangerous in the wrong hands, but it can be a powerful force for those who use it wisely. For centuries, magic has been used to aid in Healing. It can be used for everything from enhancing crop growth to expanding understanding and thinking abilities."

The sorceress made it sound so... benign. But the spy had to know. She timidly raised her hand.

"Yes?" the sorceress acknowledged her.

"If magic is so good and useful, why is it banned across most of the continent? Why do other nations think it is evil and an affront to the gods?"

"That is a wonderful question. I'm glad you asked. The answer is power."

The spy tilted her head. If the answer was power, wouldn't they want it?

"I know what you're thinking," the sorceress answered. "But it is not the nations who wanted power. The truth is, there are no gods. There is only one Creator, and he gave magic as a gift to be used. In the days before the Great War, there were many powerful, magical beings. Among those were unicorns, griffins, dragons, manticores, pegasi, and many others. But not all of them were good. They wanted more and more power, and little by little, killed one another off."

Her gaze swept toward the mountains beyond the castle to the north. "The dragons were some of the last to survive, but even they eventually all disappeared. However, there were still a few creatures who could wield magic, and they set themselves up as gods among the people. The manticore known as Kir, and the pegasus, Nyn, the triton, Veya, among others, are still worshipped today, even though they died during the Great War. They were the ones who kept people from learning magic, who declared it evil, because they wanted to be the only ones who could use it."

The sorceress sighed. "The dragons understood that the gift was not to be hoarded, but was to be shared. And so it is their legacy that I pass on to you now, to use, both in this war, but also after."

The sorceress continued talking about the history and purpose of magic, but the spy stopped listening.

Could it be true? Was magic really to be used by any who wanted?

The sorceress didn't seem evil, didn't seem vicious or vindictive. Yes, she was training them to use magic, but not to hurt, only to defend. Ryshael would surely wipe everyone in this country from existence if they were given the chance. And if that happened, magic could be lost forever.

The spy had only had a small taste of what it felt like to be filled with magic… but suddenly she couldn't fathom what the world would be like without it. For the first time in her life, she wondered if, perhaps, Ryshael was wrong.

Training

"Will you be joining us today?" Ada asked the soldier.

She still hadn't learned his name. He'd saved her life, and she'd been too preoccupied to even ask. The assassin's aim had been true—she'd have died almost instantly. Stupid. Foolish and arrogant. She'd been so wrapped up in the victory of finally being allowed to teach magic to the people that she'd grown careless. She thought they had time, that she wouldn't meet danger until Legerdemain met Ryshael on the battlefield.

She should've anticipated spies and assassins. Of course they'd come after her first. The soldier was right about that. Without her, they stood no chance. Of course they wouldn't want her to train any other magic users. Of course they'd try to kill her before she could.

She needed to be more on her guard. But he'd been there, and he'd saved her, even if he still didn't believe it.

"I... I'm on duty," he said.

"You can practice while you guard," she said.

He couldn't, and they both knew it. Someone needed their eyes open.

"That's all right," he smiled. "I can learn another time, when you're not having knives thrown at you."

Ada smiled. "Well, then, I insist you let me teach you sometime when you're not on duty. I've rarely seen such raw talent in someone untrained."

"I'm still don't believe that was me," he said.

"Why not? You've been listening to me tell others how do draw on magical energy. Magic is instinctual as much as it is trained. You anticipated the danger, and did what you needed to in order to mitigate it. You saved my life..." she paused.

"Cornan," the soldier supplied.

"Thank you. You saved my life, Cornan. Such ability will serve you well, and more so if you let me help you hone it."

"Very well. I will meet you after I am off duty, if you're not busy, and try to learn. Although I'm still not convinced I have the ability you claim."

"Don't worry," Ada said. "I'll convince you."

"I'll allow it," Cornan said, giving her a playful wink.

Heat rose to Ada's cheeks. Was she blushing? She couldn't remember ever blushing in her life, and she'd lived a long, long time.

She turned away quickly and made her way to the front of the courtyard where all the potential magic users from the Villages had gathered for their magic lesson.

Her lips twitched. She was smiling. She rarely smiled, and when she did, it was out of politeness, a social convention that was expected of her. So why did her face seem to want to smile of its own accord?

"Good morning," she said to her students. "I trust you all rested well?"

Nods and murmurs of assent rose up through the crowd.

"Very good. I would love to take the time to teach you every step of magic and every element I know. Unfortunately, we are at war. So our focus will be directed in specific areas, based on your individual strengths and talents. We will need Healers, to help the wounded on the battlefield, those who are proficient with nature to help build our defenses, and those who are able to use magic as a weapon, specifically. Today we will determine your particular strength and divide into groups."

She led them through a series of exercises to help them connect to the magical energy, and then gave them instructions in different categories, watching to determine who seemed to be more proficient with which type of magic.

By the end of the first hour, she had divided her students into three groups and given each group a specific set of instructions to practice which would help them hone and develop their talent.

By the time they took a break for lunch, most of them had mastered the first spell she'd taught them.

"Very well done," she said. "Food will be served outside the castle gates. We'll reconvene in an hour."

She slumped against a wall, watching them file from the courtyard and head toward where the smell of roast mutton and vegetables filled the air.

"My lady," Cornan said.

She turned to him, and he handed her a plate, piled high with food.

"You need to eat, too," he told her.

"I don't have time to eat," she sighed.

"You don't have a choice. The king put your wellbeing in my hands. If you don't eat, I'll be tried for treason or something."

His tone was teasing, and his eyes—oh, his eyes. How had she not noticed his eyes before? Deep, dark pools, in which she could see to his very soul. His eyes twinkled with enjoyment.

"Well, we can't have that," Ada said, matching his smile. She sat on the cobbles and lifted a bite to her mouth, then stopped, feeling suddenly awkward and having him watch her. "You should eat, too."

"Can't," he said. "I can't leave you alone. Who knows what kind of danger you'll put yourself in?"

"Well, don't just sit there and watch me eat. Go... look for threats or something."

He laughed, a deep, rich sound that filled the courtyard. Dimples dug deep into both of his cheeks, visible despite the neatly trimmed beard that grew along his jaw.

"Your word is my command, my lady," he said.

He turned and stood in a protective stance, his head turning in a slow arc as he scanned the courtyard for non-existent threats.

She quickly finished her meal, then stood and joined him in his perusal of the courtyard. "Thank you for keeping me safe," she said. She nodded toward a flock of chickens that pecked for bugs in an alley. "You never know what those things may be capable of."

"I'm here to help," he grinned.

The first of the students filtered around the corner, coming back to where his group had met.

"What will you teach them now?" Cornan asked.

"Both as much and as little as I can. The scouts say the army is gathering on the other side of the river, just outside Ryshael's borders."

"What of Cadalania and Kir?"

"We have sent messengers to both, requesting aid, but I doubt we'll receive any help. Both nations, I suspect, are waiting like vultures to scoop up whatever they can after the war. If we win, they'll devour

Ryshael between them, and if we lose, then they'll make their treaties with Ryshael to avoid the same fate."

Cornan's beautiful smile hardened into a thin line. "Then we'd better not lose."

Soldier

Cornan stood in the empty courtyard. Dusk had fallen, and a chill swept across the cobbles. Other soldiers were on duty, guarding the castle, and guarding the hallways near Ada. When the king heard about the assassin, he'd insisted on a nonstop guard around Ada.

Cornan would've volunteered for every shift, if it had been possible. As it was, however, he was limited to just during the day, when she was training her apprentices.

The king himself even came out with his personal guard occasionally, so extra eyes would be on-hand if there was any trouble while Ada was exposed.

But at the moment, she was safe inside, presumably eating her dinner or mixing up potions in her rooms, and Cornan had until the next morning to himself. He closed his eyes and breathed in deeply, focusing on the light that seemed to be glowing all around him. He'd heard Ada's instructions so many times, it was easy to follow them, even though she wasn't near.

He pulled on the light, and made it into a candle, the way she had instructed. It was so easy—how was it possible that so many of the apprentices took hours to accomplish something so simple?

He then concentrated on some of the other things he'd heard Ada say—focus on a rock or a tree and imagine that thing bending or moving, then using the light to move it. Imagining something broken and using the light to fix it. Imagining the light as a gust of wind…

"I thought you were going to let me teach you."

Cornan dropped the ball of light that had formed in his hand and whirled around.

Ada leaned against the archway that led from the courtyard to the stables, her soft, red lips turned up in a smile.

"You are teaching me," he said, returning the smile.

"You believe me, then?" she asked.

Cornan dropped his hands. He could create the things she said so easily. But it couldn't be. He could not have used magic without realizing it. She must have been the one to do the spell to stop the knife. But if so, why did she insist that he'd saved her life?

"I don't know what I believe."

"But you know now you can use magic. Which exercise was easiest for you?"

"I don't know. They all seemed simple."

"Then what do you want to do with magic? If you could use it for anything, what would you use it for?"

"To make me a better soldier."

Ada smiled. "Then that's what we will focus on."

We. For some reason, that word lodged in his mind, filling him with warmth. We. Like they were a team. A unit.

"How do we do that?"

"You were there, during the first battle. Before the battle began, I sent strength and healing through you, to help keep you from becoming fatigued and to protect against being wounded. You can do the same for yourself. Focus on the magical energy—that ball of light—and think of it as raw power, pure strength, and a barrier between you and your enemy.

Cornan closed his eyes.

"You don't have to close your eyes. I just start people out that way because they tend to focus better when they can't see what is going on around them. But eventually you'll want to be able to draw on magic without losing sight of your surroundings. You, I think, will have no problem."

Cornan opened his eyes and focused on her face as he pulled magic into himself, drawing on the light—the strength and power.

"Good," Ada said. "Now, infuse that power into yourself. Make it a part of you. Create a shield to cover your whole body."

Cornan did as she instructed.

"Perfect. Now, imagine it settling there and staying. It will wear off eventually, but the spell should last you through a battle, at any rate. Tell it to stay, and you shouldn't have to worry about it, leaving your mind free to begin a new spell."

Cornan imagined the shield of light becoming part of him, wrapping around him and forming a shell over his entire body, protecting him from all harm.

"Now, let's practice forming a weapon. Magic is a tool, and it can be shaped in any way you choose, but it is easier and more efficient the less you have to force it. I like to use lightning. The currents are already in the air, so it's just a matter of drawing them together and focusing them in a particular direction."

"I… I don't know what a good weapon would be. I'm most efficient with a sword, but…"

"Then make a sword. Or imbue your own sword with magical energy so that it is more lethal."

"Let's start with that," Cornan said. "How do I do that?"

"Light and heat are almost always available. Draw on the light and heat, and instead of feeding it into yourself, like you did with the protection spell, feed it into your sword."

Cornan pulled on the light and felt it warm as it passed through him, but every time he tried to push it into the sword, it dissipated.

He tried several times, but the magic refused to bend to his will.

"This isn't going to work," he grumbled.

"You're trying too hard to force it. It can be forced, but it takes a lot of practice and expends a lot of energy. Let me help." Ada placed a hand on top of his on the hilt of his sword. "Draw the light in."

He obeyed.

"Feel it flow through you, into your fingertips."

His hand tingled at her touch.

"The sword is an extension of your hand. The energy wants to go into it. That is where it belongs. It wants to flow through you as freely as your blood, and through the sword like it is your body. Let it be free."

His hand warmed, and the hilt began to feel hot, but not too hot to hold. Prickles like tiny shocks skittered across his skin. Ada's hand warmed, and tingles flowed from her into him, then pushed out through his hand and into the sword.

The blade glowed, like it was fresh from the forge, brilliant and sharp, a blade of light.

"Good," Ada murmured. "Keep it flowing." She slowly drew her hand away.

The magic in the sword flickered for a moment, but Cornan kept it going, and managed to steady it.

48

Ada nodded toward a log on the ground. "Cut through it. Get a feel for how the sword moves. It will be similar, but just enough different that you'll want to practice with it often."

Cornan sliced through the log. The magical blade sliced through it like running it through a loaf of soft bread.

"It works!" he grinned, turning to face Ada.

"Very good, she smiled. She stretched out her hands and a sword of glowing light—pure magic—formed in her grip. "Now, practice using it in combat."

She lunged, forcing him to parry her strike. He worried for half an instant that he would hurt her, but her smooth, graceful movements and steady arm quickly proved her to be easily his equal. He grinned. This was going to be fun.

Student

King Ondrei looked out over the courtyard from the window in his study. He was supposed to be planning a strategy, but he couldn't concentrate.

Ada was down there, teaching someone magic. She'd been teaching magic all day, and he could see in her eyes at dinner just how much it exhausted her. So why was she down there now, teaching someone else? He ought to impose his will on her. Force her to stop overextending herself. He needed her to be strong, at her peak.

What was she doing now? Sword fighting?

Was that man trying to kill her? She was supposed to be guarded! Where were her escorts?

He started to call out to his personal guards, but stopped. Ada had her attacker at her mercy, the blade of her magical sword at his throat.

A musical laugh rang out, its tinkling echoing through the courtyard. She took a step back from the attacker and readied her sword. The man did the same, settling into a fighting stance, and a moment later, their swords clashed again.

Ada moved fluidly, her body dancing back and forth, in and out as she sparred with the soldier. He was a soldier, Ondrei now realized. And he also wielded a magical sword, though not the same as Ada's.

This was good. If all the soldiers had magical swords, the Ryshaelans wouldn't stand a chance.

What would it take for her to make lots of those swords?

The match ended—the soldier won, that time—and both Ada and the soldier leaned against the wall, presumably to catch their breath. The soldier stood just a little closer than Ondrei appreciated. Not inappropriately close, but still, too close. He'd have to keep a close watch on the man. But in the meantime, he needed to talk to Ada about getting those swords for the army.

He called to the guard at the door. "Summon Ada, please. She's in the courtyard."

The guard bowed, then turned to do Ondrei's bidding.

Ada and the soldier started another match, which Ada was winning until the guard burst out into the courtyard and hailed her.

Ondrei couldn't see her face, but her body seemed to immediately tense, losing the easy, unconscious grace she'd had while sparring, and taking on a rigid, formal pose. The magical sword dissipated and she followed the guard through the gate.

Ondrei glanced once more at the soldier. The glow on his sword began to fade, leaving him with an ordinary battle sword. So, regular swords could be charged with magic, making them more powerful? That was brilliant. And much easier, he imagined, than creating an entire magical armory.

Ada arrived a few minutes later. "You wished to see me, your majesty?"

"I saw you outside. Without a guard." He tried to keep his tone from sounding too accusatory, but the flash of annoyance that crossed her face told him he'd failed.

"I was with a guard."

"Yes, but you should have a full escort with you at all times. What if something should happen to you? The kingdom needs you." He paused. "*I* need you."

"Well, here I am. What did you want to see me about?"

Ondrei frowned. He'd hoped for some sort of acknowledgement, at least, at his admission, but Ada seemed not to even notice that he'd expressed anything out of the ordinary. "You were sparring with him. Using magical swords."

"Yes."

"Can you make all the soldiers' swords magical, like you did for that one?"

"I didn't make his magical. He did."

"The soldier has magical ability?"

Ada nodded.

"Then can you teach the others?"

Ada's brows furrowed, ever so slightly, as she paused, looking for the right words. "I will teach anyone who wishes to learn. However, I would advise you not to put too much hope into having a magical army at your disposal. Such talent in a soldier is very, very rare."

"Why should it be any more rare in soldiers than in the general population? Surely there must be some who possess the talent."

"I'm sure there are some. However, soldiers rely heavily on their training. They work to make their bodies and minds conform to their demands. They practice great discipline and structure. Magic is about surrendering and letting a force outside your body control you as much as you control it. Even if they have the talent, it would take a great deal of un-training to be able to access it."

"But that soldier did."

"Yes."

"So you will teach the others. As many as you can."

Ada bowed. "I'll begin in the morning testing for ability. Was there anything else?"

She was going to leave. The whole room seemed brighter for having her in it, and the thought of her dismissing him without so much as a thought sent a pang through him.

"One more thing," he said.

She clasped her hands in front of her and waited for him to speak.

"You always say that the royal line is gifted with great magical ability. That my grandfather before me, and his mother before him, back to the beginning of the nation, were powerful sorcerers."

"That's right. Your father refused to learn. He had a mistress, before he married your mother, a refugee from Sunnland, who told him the horrors of how her land had been ravaged by magic users for generations, and how it had devastated everything from the economy to the natural landscape to the political climate, and that was why magic was banned entirely from their country. Your father feared what would happen if magic was allowed to be used freely."

"But magic has never been practiced widely, even here."

"True," Ada nodded. "Even before your father, only the elite were trained in magic use, a rule that was passed down from the beginning of the nation because of the havoc on the earth after the war. But that was not the ideal the kingdom was founded on, or the intent of the First King."

"And you think I have the same magical powers they did?"

"I know you do."

Ondrei took a deep breath, to steady himself and confirm his resolve. "Then I would like to learn. Not just for myself, but for my kingdom."

Ada nodded. "That is a wise decision, your Majesty. When would you like to begin?"

Ondrei smiled, a deep sense of satisfaction settling over him. "Immediately."

"Very well. In that case, close your eyes."

Boulders

Swords of light clashed against one another, sending sparks flying in the twilight. One landed in a pile of hay next to the wall.

Ada held up her hand, to pause the match, and directed a wave of magic to snuff out the flame.

"I wish I could see what you were doing when you do spells," Cornan said. "It would make it much easier to replicate."

"There is a lot to be said for the ability to use your imagination," Ada smiled. "But come here."

She let her light sword dissolve and held out her hand to him.

He took it, sending a rush of warmth through her. She pushed aside the feeling—that was not what she wanted him to sense through her.

"Focus on the magic. You should be able to sense it when I draw it into me—you should be able to feel the way it changes form."

She drew energy from the air and formed it in her mind into a sort of cloudburst, a pillow of water and air, then directed its flow to the haystack and released it.

It was imperceptible to the human eye, but the effect was as if she'd dumped a bucket of water on the hay.

"I see what you did," Cornan muttered, his eyes still closed. He kept hold on her hand while he duplicated her action. It wasn't exact, but it was fairly close. It achieved the same result, but with Cornan's own unique flair to it.

He opened his eyes and grinned at her. "I did it!"

His enthusiasm reminded her of a child's. And yet he was not the least bit childlike. He was older than Ondrei by at least a decade. Gray streaked his beard and hair, and the raw power of years of training and defending the throne emanated from every part of him.

His eyes had softened, and he grinned again, this time a teasing, almost seductive grin. "I agree."

And he still held her hand.

She pulled away. "What?"

He reached for her hand again. "You know what."

She quickly cloaked herself in her typical aloof demeanor. "I don't know what you're talking about."

"Yes you do. You forget, when there is magic flowing through us, we're connected. I know what you were thinking."

"Oh? And what was that?"

"How much you wanted me to kiss you."

She yanked her hand away. "I most certainly was not."

He stepped closer. "I know. But you are now."

She threw up her hands in exaggerated exasperation. "Honestly, is that all men think about? We're trying to prepare for a war, and all you can do is bring up kissing."

His rich, deep laugh rumbled across the courtyard. "You were the one thinking it, not me."

She crossed her arms in front of her chest, feeling like a petulant child. "If you're not going to take your lessons seriously, then I'm not going to waste my time teaching you."

"My apologies," he said. He stepped back and readied his magical sword—he'd learned to create one, in addition to empowering his steel sword, so in case he lost his sword, he said, he'd always have one at the ready—but his eyes still held that mischievous twinkle. "Shall we?"

She created her own magical sword and bowed to him.

They sparred for a few more rounds before they were both in need of a rest.

Ada leaned against the wall to catch her breath, and Cornan moved to stand beside her.

"This is good for hand-to-hand combat, but I need to learn more. We're so desperately outnumbered—I need to learn spells that will wipe out more than one enemy at a time." His hand found hers.

She almost pulled away, but the action felt so benign—friendly camaraderie rather than attempted seduction.

She let her hand rest in his. "You can do virtually anything if you can imagine it. What do you want to do?"

"I don't know. I haven't imagined it yet."

She laughed. "Let's go out of the city and try some things."

Still holding his hand, she led the way down the main thoroughfare to the field that surrounded the city.

The night was bright in the rising moon, and Ada, her vision enhanced by the magic flowing through her, could see the dip where the Wyvern River cut, to the southwest, far in the distance.

"Reach out with magic. Feel the world around you. Feel the connection."

She waited, feeling Cornan's energy as it connected to everything else. "Focus on something in the distance."

His attention narrowed, and Ada followed the flow to a large boulder in the field beyond.

"Good. You're connected to the boulder. Now, what do you want to do with it?"

She felt his mental energy, like muscles flexing, as he harnessed the magic.

A moment later, the boulder exploded.

She gasped and dropped his hand.

"Did I do something wrong?" he asked.

"No, not at all. That was... powerful. More than I imagined you were capable of yet. You have so much talent. Do it again."

He obeyed, each explosion larger than the last.

Something moved behind them, and Ada whirled around.

A young woman—one of her new recruits—stood there, gaping.

"I'm—I'm sorry. I didn't mean to... I saw you leave and I was just curious."

Ada smiled. "It's quite all right... I'm sorry, I don't remember your name."

The girl took a step closer. "Elya," she said. She looked at Cornan. "How are you doing that?"

"I don't really know," he told her. "But I think I can teach you." He extended his hand, and Elya took it.

"Do you feel that boulder?"

Elya nodded.

The boulder exploded and Elya jumped.

"Can... can I do that, too?" she asked.

Ada nodded. "You can do anything you can think of, if you can concentrate hard enough. Connect to the earth. Feel it. Focus on it. Find what you're looking for."

Elya closed her eyes. In the distance, a tiny puff of dirt and rocks signified her replication of the spell.

"I did it!" she jumped up, excitement shining from her face.

"You did," Ada smiled. "Very well done. Magic can be used to destroy, as well as to create. You can use those same manipulations to change the course of rivers or to knit someone's skin together after an injury. The same powers used in war can be used to rebuild. That's what we're fighting for. We're fighting to protect ourselves and our ability to be free, and to use magic to build and heal, not just destroy."

Elya nodded solemnly. She closed her eyes, and a few more puffs of dust, getting increasingly larger, showed her progress.

"Very well done," Ada said after awhile. "Now, go on back. We have a lot of work to do over the next few days, and you need your rest."

Elya curtsied and hurried back toward the city.

Cornan took Ada's hand again. "What do you think our chances are, really?"

Ada sighed and leaned her head against his shoulder. "If everyone learned as quickly and had as much power and control as you, or even as her, we might stand a chance. As it is... I wish I knew."

Cornan turned slightly and slipped his free arm around her waist, pulling her into an embrace and resting his head on top of hers.

For the first time in longer than she remembered, she felt comfortable. Peaceful. Hopeful.

Cornan grinned—she could feel it in the way his jaw shifted on the top of her head. "You're thinking about kissing me again, aren't you?"

Mountains

"Are they ready?" Ondrei asked.

Ada clenched her fists, then willed herself to relax. "No. I could train them for a decade and they still wouldn't be ready. But we're out of time. Scouts say more troops join Ryshael every day. Very soon they'll advance, and when they do, we need to be ready."

Ondrei turned from the window where he looked out on the fields that were just beginning to turn golden in the morning light. "What is our next step, then?"

"I will go with the earth movers to the mountains and teach them what they must do to change the course of the tributaries. Are the construction crews ready to build the dam?"

Ondrei nodded.

"We will have to use magic for that, as well. Otherwise it will take too long."

Ondrei took a step closer to her. "I don't understand why *you* have to go. The mountains are treacherous."

Ada sighed. The time of keeping the mountains sacred was past. "The mountains aren't dangerous. That story was told about a hundred years ago to keep people out of them."

"I don't understand. Why would anyone want to keep people out of the mountains?"

"Sacred beings lived there. Beings that did not want to be disturbed. Rumors were planted to keep people from wanting to explore."

"But we're going to disturb them now."

Ada sighed. "They're long gone, now. Anything that was left of them has died or disappeared, and may or may not ever return."

"But people have gone exploring—and have disappeared. Surely if they'd gone and been safe, we would've heard about it before and people would've migrated there."

"There are certain... protections that were put in place. Spells that, when triggered, could cause someone to lose their memory or become ill. Protections which I can dismantle."

Ondrei stared at her as if she'd sprouted a third eye. "Why would you lie about something like this?"

"My reasons go far beyond you or your reign. But I made certain promises, one of which was to protect this land at all costs. Now, fulfilling that promise requires entrance into the mountains, and supersedes other promises I made long ago."

Ondrei's features softened. "Just when I think I know all there is to know about you."

She scoffed. "You know even less than you think you do about me."

He smiled and stepped closer again. "And yet every new thing I learn makes me admire you more."

She stepped away before he could decide to act on the intentions playing out in his eyes.

"I must go. I'll get the sorcerers started and be back in two days."

She strode from the throne room and went down to the stable.

Those sorcerers who she had designated to be in the group going to the mountains hovered close to one another, pulling cloaks tighter around themselves in the cold morning air. The gate opened and the troop of construction workers came through with their wagons of supplies.

"Let's go," Ada said.

The construction crew and the designated group of sorcerers mounted their horses, and Ada led the way through the city to the North Gate. By lunch, they'd arrived at the North Village. After a short break, they turned to the northeast. Ada had decided the Sapphire River was more vital to the plan than the Wyvern, so they'd start there, and then she would take part of the group to the west, to the head of the Wyvern.

They arrived at the foothills, where the first tributary ran down from the east and joined the Sapphire, just before sundown. Ada assigned some to make camp while others began using magic to chop down trees and create a lumber supply for building the dam until the darkness and their weariness made it impossible to continue.

They began work at dawn, the construction workers using some of the sorcerers to help lift and carry to make the building go faster.

"I'll be back in a little bit," she said.

She walked uphill for awhile, along an old game trail that led up onto the mountain. The cold air bit at her skin, but she didn't mind. This mountain was home, in a way that the city could never be. She closed her eyes and breathed deeply of the pine-scented air. She thought about her family, long-since gone, and the promises she'd made to them.

"I hope it has been long enough," she whispered. "I hope that what I must do now does not disturb your rest."

She reached out and pulled magic into herself, then felt along the mountain ridges until she felt the spell that waited for someone to trip it.

It was already faded—its potency less than a quarter what it had been when it was put in place. Originally, it would've sent a jolt like lightning through whoever triggered it, incapacitating them long enough that they would die of exposure or be attacked by a wild animal before they could get to safety. Now, it was just strong enough to give a startling zap.

Still, she could not afford for the people to be harmed, even by this small of a spell.

She moved along the mountain trails, disarming spells as she went until she'd cleared a long swath, then went back to where the sorcerers worked on the dam.

She assigned a few of them to stay and help, then beckoned to the others. "The rest of you, with me."

She led ten sorcerers across the river and further into the mountains. Before long, they came to a small river that wound down from the mountains and disappeared somewhere to the east.

"We are going to redirect this river into the Sapphire," she said.

Using magic, she moved the earth, creating a pit just a few feet from the riverbank that stretched into a shallow ravine as she moved toward the Sapphire.

She took the hands of two of the sorcerers so they could feel her magic and showed them how to move the dirt. "It needs to be deeper, wider, and stretch down to the Sapphire. Keep working here. When the channels are complete and we are ready to use this as a barrier, then we will finish the last bit to connect it to this river, and use the dirt to dam up the other path, so the water is forced into this channel."

She took the next group further up into the mountains until they reached a creek. Leaving behind two sorcerers at a time to create the channels, she kept moving on to different rivers and streams, instructing them to meet her back at the camp when they finished.

By the time she returned, the dam was almost complete, surrounded by a pit which would become a large pond when the water filled it, and with a pulley system that could raise and lower the various vents in the side of the dam to release more or less water as needed.

She gathered all the people to her.

"In the morning, most of us will depart to the Wyvern river in the west and do the same thing. I need a few volunteers to stay here and continue on. We need as many tributaries redirected into these rivers as possible. You will need to expand the basin, as well. Make it deeper so it can hold more. Make it into a lake, if you need to."

"My lady!" one of the sorcerers called. "My lady, look!" He held an amethyst above his head. Raw, uncut, but just enough chipped away from the outside to see the flash of purple in the evening light. "I found it in the riverbed after we changed the course of one of the rivers."

Ada smiled, even as tears stung her eyes. "Keep it. If you direct magic through it, it becomes even more powerful."

"Are there more?" someone else asked.

"Probably," she answered. "I suspect in years to come, we will find vast amounts of gemstones to be mined in these mountains."

"Why is that?" the first one asked.

A pang stabbed at her. "Gemstones can be mined from most mountains, if you know where to look. But there is a legend that dragons once roamed these hills. The legend says that when a dragon dies, its body turns into jewels, which is why gems are so potent in magic use."

"Is the legend true?"

Ada smiled. "I like to believe it is."

Stars

Ada lay in the field, looking up at the stars. She'd returned from the Wyvern earlier in the day, where she'd left sorcerers to do the same there as they'd done on the east with the Sapphire.

The icy ground seeped into her, chilling her throughout, but she ignored it. She couldn't sleep. She knew she should be resting as much as possible, but so much hinged on this war.

She had to believe they would win. But what if they didn't? The prophecies didn't actually state that they would. That it would be Legerdemain that stood between the world and utter evil. Certain things were set in stone. That a great evil would come from across the ocean and threaten everyone, and that the child of the dragons would be the one who would conquer—that much was certain.

But one prophecy also said that the child would be lost. What if now was when the line was lost? What if Legerdemain ceased to exist? How would she find that child and protect it until the prophecy could be fulfilled?

And what if it wasn't her destiny at all? Perhaps they were wrong when they Saw her role in this kingdom.

She could be killed. The child of the prophecy might not even be born for centuries. Who knew what could happen between now and then?

A footstep crunched on the frosted grass, and she looked up.

Warmth flooded her despite the cold. Cornan.

"I thought I saw you come out here. What are you doing?" he asked.

"Thinking."

"Does freezing to death help with that?"

She gave a small laugh. "Sometimes."

He took off his cloak and spread it out on the ground, then lay on top of it. "Come here," he said.

She joined him on the cloak and looked back up at the sky.

His hand brushed hers, and she accepted the gesture, intertwining her fingers with his. With her other hand, she pointed to the constellations burning in the night sky. "See that one? That's known as the Sea Witch. It's said she and the Hunter stalk one another, and their movements control the ocean's tempests."

"Is it true?"

She shrugged. "I think it's more about looking in the past than in the future, honestly. There are some things that can be predicted, but the movement of the stars doesn't shape the future, it only explains it."

"So the stars can't tell us if we'll win this war?"

She snorted. "If only. I've been staring at them for hours and all I see are stars. I have tried to use magic to See what will come, but I only See the fighting, not the outcome."

"So you can't See the part where you and I fall madly in love and live together forever."

She laughed, a real laugh this time. "I definitely do not see that."

He pointed to the Pegasus. This time of year, her wings were spread as though she was in flight. "Do you know what I see? That's us. Running away after we win the war. Just the two of us."

She shifted so she was a little closer to him, absorbing his warmth. "I wish I could see that."

"Do you?" His voice held a note of wistfulness.

"We should get inside. It's not warm enough to be out here. Besides, we have a war to start in the morning."

"Ever the optimist, aren't you?"

"It's part of the job."

"And what job is that, exactly? The royal midwife? Advisor to the king? Chief sorceress?"

"All that and more."

"Now, *that* I believe. You are so much more than any description could possibly cover."

She'd been told more or less the same thing countless times before, so why did it mean something different from him?

He squeezed her hand. "Ada."

She turned to look at him, their faces close, his breath warming her cheeks. Her breath caught and she had to consciously look him in the eye so her gaze didn't wander to his lips. "What is it?" she asked.

"I'm serious. About running away together."

She started to speak, but he silenced her with a finger to her lips. "I know you can't. I know that there is more to you than I can ever understand, and that your duty to the king and the country comes first. But whatever happens tomorrow, I wanted to make sure you know. If there's ever a chance, I'll be waiting for you."

Tears stung her eyes.

It could never be. But in that moment, she wished, for the first time in over a hundred years, that things could be different.

Cornan pulled away and rolled to his feet. "It's cold out here. Why'd you keep me out this long?"

She giggled like a child as she took the hand he extended to her to help her up. "I just wanted to see if you were as tough as you pretend to be."

His eyes twinkled in the moonlight. "And?"

"I suppose you're tough enough. Like an old goat."

"Exactly what I was going for."

He kept hold of her hand as they trudged back to the castle. They walked in silence for awhile, until Cornan spoke.

"What's in the mountains?"

"What do you mean?"

For as long as I can remember, people have been afraid to go near the mountains. Stories my grandmother told me, that were told to her by her grandmother, passed down for generations, about how we must never venture too far. But now we have people there, working on the rivers and dams, with no ill consequence."

Ada sighed, a pang almost as deep as the one she felt when she thought about the future she'd never have with Cornan shooting through her. "There's nothing there anymore. Once, a long time ago, it was said that dragons lived among us. When their time came to leave the world of men, they went into the mountains to hibernate until the end of time. The prophecies say that at the end of this age, they will return to bring peace and justice."

"If they're hibernating, why would people be afraid to go into the mountains?"

Ada smiled. "It was for their protection, not man's. While they sleep, they're vulnerable. They put up magical protections, wards against people so their caves would not be found."

"And those are gone now?"

Ada nodded. "What wards were left were so weak, they were nearly inconsequential. If there were dragons, they're no longer protected anyway. I removed the wards so our people would be safe, but at this point... the dragons are all long since dead, I'm sure."

"And you don't think they'll return at the end of the age, like the prophecies say?"

Ada exhaled. "I don't know. I hope they will, but... I just don't know."

The Army

"The scouts say the Ryshaelan army is on the move. They'll be within our borders by tomorrow night at the latest." The messenger looked uncertainly between Ada and King Ondrei, not sure who he should be addressing.

Ada nodded at him. "How many?"

"Too many to count, my lady. A hundred thousand, at least."

"Tell the captain of the army to assemble the troops on the plain south of the South Village. Evacuate the South Village."

The messenger hurried away and Ada turned to the man she had put in charge of the river project, Hovyn. "How are the rivers?"

"The dams are built, one on either side of the kingdom. The last dove I received said the channels are nearly complete, so all that is left is to redirect the flow of the tributaries into the new channels so they feed into the main rivers. The dam is equipped with machinery that will allow us to control the flow of the water."

"Good. Send a dove and have them complete the last step. As soon as possible, I want the dams opened completely and the water flowing. Let's see if we can make it a little harder for the Ryshaelans to cross our borders."

Hovyn bowed and left his seat at the table.

Ada turned to the woman who sat next to Hovyn, Beactri. "Ladies and gentlemen this is Beactri. She was the primary Healer in the West Village until she came to learn more magic. Her skill with magic is one of the strongest I've seen. Between that and her ability to lead others and stay calm in crisis, I have seen fit to delegate to her the sorcerers who have shown an ability to wield magic as a weapon. Beactri, you and

66

those under your command will go with the army. Intersperse yourselves among them."

Beactri stood and bowed, then glided away to the courtyard where already the sounds of soldiers and horses drifted through the throne room window.

Next to Beactri sat Gerdwin. "Gerdwin is the head of the Healers. Gerdwin, take your Healers, even the ones who have barely shown any ability, and follow the army. Stay back, out of harm's way, but be ready for the wounded. Heal as quickly and as efficiently as possible. We're going to need all our men fighting again as soon as possible. We can't afford to lose any to illness or infection."

Gerdwin bowed and obeyed.

Ada had spent the last few days assigning all her recruits to various groups, forming a hierarchy, and instructing them in her duties. She wanted to go with each group individually and oversee it, but she couldn't. Her place was fighting alongside her king. She had to trust that the training she'd given was enough.

"Your Majesty?" she said.

"Yes?" Ondrei asked.

"What have we learned from our prisoner, the one who tried to assassinate me?"

"Very little, and yet much. Jando has no intention of taking us alive. He will wipe us out and establish an outpost of his own people here. Perhaps use our castle for a summer home. But the assassin didn't know when Jando was planning to move or what other plans he has beyond brute force."

"You're certain he doesn't know more and is just hiding it?"

Ondrei winced, as though remembering something very unpleasant. "I'm sure."

Ada nodded, choking back the knowledge of what they would've done to be certain. "Very well. I have given all the orders I can. Carry on."

Ondrei nodded an took his turn handing out instructions to those on his Council, until one by one the room was emptied as they all went to do as they'd been ordered.

At last, only Onrdrei and Ada remained.

Ondrei reached out to take her hand, but she turned to study the map, pretending she hadn't seen.

"First thing in the morning, I'll ride out to meet the army," Ondrei said.

"I'll be with you."

Ondrei started to pull the amulet from around his neck. "You should take this."

Ada held up a hand to stop him. "It will be much more powerful in your hands."

"You are the most powerful sorceress alive. I cannot possibly do with it what you can."

"I have my own tools and artifacts. That one is yours, imbued with magic and tied directly to you through your bloodline. I can wield it, but it is yours. I showed you how to create a shield to protect yourself, and how to use magic to enhance your weapons. But if you will let it, the amulet will do so much more—*you* will do more through it. Trust me, it is better for you to keep it."

"I do trust you," Ondrei said.

The note of wistfulness in his voice made her wince. "I need to go prepare. I'll see you in the courtyard at dawn."

She hurried to her rooms, located much too close to his, but where they'd always been. After the war, she'd move her rooms to the lower level, where she could be further away from anyone and have a little more freedom of movement.

For now, though, she began filling a bag with potions and gemstones. It had to be light enough to carry on the battlefield while still containing everything she might need.

She prepared a second bag of potions and Healing herbs to deliver to the Healers who would be waiting on the battlefield. She'd taught them to make a few, but there simply hadn't been time to fully prepare for a war.

The rest of the night she spent in fitful sleep, and awoke before dawn. She dressed in black pants and a tunic and wrapped a dark cloak around her shoulders. She slung her bag over her back and carried the other bag to attach to her saddle.

The king was already waiting for her when she arrived in the courtyard. His face was drawn and puffed bags circled his eyes.

"You couldn't sleep either?" she asked.

He shook his head. "We're not ready for this war."

"No, we're not. But we don't have another choice."

Within moments, the horses were saddled, and Ada rode with Ondrei and his personal guard out of the city gates, past the empty South Village, and to the plain where the army was already assembled in formation, waiting for the enemy to strike.

Ada diverted long enough give the bag of Healing supplies to Gerdwin. He nodded his thanks, a grim frown marring his features.

She wanted to say something, to encourage him—to encourage all of them—but there was nothing to say. They could not surrender or they'd be overwhelmed. Destroyed. Everything they knew and loved, the peace and tranquility that defined their nation would be gone and they'd be slaves to the Ryshaelan empire, which would use them and their skills to engage in yet more conquest.

But this battle would not be won easily. Even if they prevailed, many would die.

Over the distant hills, beyond the river, flashes of sunlight glinted on the armor of the first Ryshaelan soldiers to come into view. A few moments later, they began to ford the river.

Ada closed her eyes and felt out with her mind, touching the earth, the sky, the river.

The river swelled, but the onslaught was too far north as yet. She sent magic through the earth to the river, urging it along.

The first wave of the Ryshaelan army was across the river, thundering toward them. The Legerdemainian army readied their weapons.

A crack like thunder echoed through the valley.

Ada smiled. The river had come.

The surge of water swept away a huge mass of riders who were still in the middle of the river, sending them tumbling downriver. Even if they survived—and most of them wouldn't—it would be hours before they could return to the main force.

The water also effectively cut off those who had already crossed from the rest of the army. They were still outnumbered, but at least they stood a chance against this smaller force, and could cut them down before the rest found a way across the river.

Ondrei looked at her, and she nodded.

He raised his sword in the air, signaling his men to attack.

Rescue

Cornan edged his horse to the front of the army. He created the magical shield for himself, and lanced his sword with magic.

The king had done the same. When had Ada taught him that? Had she spent as much time with the king as she'd spent with Cornan? Time with just the two of them, close together, touching as she showed him how to work the spells?

He'd seen the way the king looked at Ada, with that unabashed longing in his eyes...

He shoved the thought away. This was no time for petty jealousy. They could use every ounce of magic that they could produce, including and especially wielded by the king. The king using magic would strike fear into the enemy and increase motivation among the sorcerers scattered through the ranks.

Cornan glanced back to find Ada. The woman moved like a bird, flitting back and forth seemingly without direction. He knew that wasn't true, though—Ada did nothing without thinking it through first. She was the most infernally cautious woman he'd ever met—and yet also the most brilliant. Her understanding of military strategy would be impressive in the most hardened war veteran, but coming from a woman of her age...

Then again, he actually had no idea how old she was. She looked to be a young woman in her prime, but her eyes were much older, and some of the things she said...

The first of the Ryshaelans connected with the first Legerdemainian soldier, and an instant later both sides crashed into one another, swords clashing as they slashed each other down.

Cornan rode forward, his magic-imbued sword blazing. It sliced cleanly through one soldier and then another. He pushed forward, into their ranks, trusting on instinct to guide his sword as he mentally searched the earth for a boulder of sufficient size.

He found one, and sent magic into it, causing it to explode outward in the midst of the Ryshaelan army, killing or wounding the half-dozen men closest to it.

Again and again, he found rocks in the field and destroyed them.

It seemed like hours, though he knew it was only minutes, when his body began to feel the strain of wielding that much magic.

His limbs felt heavy and his mind slowed, making it harder to focus, to react, to draw on magic to do the next spell.

And still the Ryshaelans pushed forward. He needed to rest, but he couldn't afford to.

All he wanted was to sleep, to let the heaviness in his head take over, but he couldn't allow his eyes to close. If they closed, he'd be dead. Worse, others would die.

Ada might die.

A Ryshaelan rider broke off from the main force, dodging the Legerdemainian soldiers as he cut his way toward something—or someone—to Cornan's left.

Cornan glanced along his trajectory.

The rider headed straight toward Ada, as she rode along the front lines, fighting the enemy with bolts of lightning from her fingertips.

Of course it would be her. As much as the king—and maybe even more—she was the one who would keep the army motivated and the kingdom intact. If they killed her, they destroyed the morale that would keep Legerdemain fighting. If they killed Ada, Legerdemain would fall. The Ryshaelans understood that as clearly as Cornan did.

Pushing the fog from his mind, he yanked his reins, forcing his horse Ada's direction, hoping to intersect with her attacker. Ryshaelans closed in around them, but he refused to let them stop him, slicing down any who crossed his path.

The rider drew ever close to Ada, pulling a lance as he rode.

Ada was facing the other way, her attention focused on the river. She wouldn't see the assassin. He would drive the lance straight through her.

Cornan hadn't really believed Ada when she'd told him he was the one who stopped the knife during the first assassination attempt.

He could use magic, but that… that was something else.

And yet… he wouldn't reach her in time. There were too many others in the way, and the rider was going too fast. He'd seen Ada do things, unbelievable things. He could do this.

He had to do this, or she would die. And if she died, no matter how the war turned out, he wouldn't be able to live.

He drew magic into himself, pushing past the exhaustion and the fear and the uncertainty until he felt like he would explode from the power of it. He formed it in his mind, into a ball of fire and energy and let it fly toward the rider.

The whole earth erupted as the fireball hit the rider, sending him tumbling in a mass of flames and screams, into a clump of his compatriots.

Ada turned sharply, seeing the pyre that formed of the bodies of men and horses, then turned to see Cornan.

The look of alarm softened and she rode toward him.

Cornan slumped in his saddle, scarcely able to keep his eyes open.

Ada pulled up alongside him and touched his face. Warmth from her fingertips seeped into him pushing away the exhaustion and filling him with renewed energy.

He sat up straighter and blinked. He would have to learn how to do that.

Though he felt as fresh as the morning dew, Ada didn't remove her hand from his face. Her touch swept across the beard on his jaw, feeling almost like a caress, and she gazed up at him.

"That's the second time you've saved me from assassination," she said. "I owe you."

He grinned down at her. "Is that right?"

"Don't get your hopes up. I'm still not thinking about kissing you." She pulled her hand away, but a smile quirked the corner of her lips, and he could swear the flush in her cheeks was from more than exertion.

"Let's win this battle, and then I'll change your mind on that," he said.

The grin overtook her face, making it light up like a jewel in the sun. "When we win this war, I'll let you try."

She turned her horse and sped away, and he refocused on the oncoming horde. This was no time to be thinking about kissing… but thinking about kissing Ada was the one thing that kept him fighting.

The Forest

Lightning flashed and swords clashed as the Ryshaelan army pushed the Legerdemainians back, little by little. Before long, they'd be driven into the South Village. Already, farms had been destroyed all along the southern stretch of the country.

The sorcerers lanced the enemy with magic, but like insects, they crawled over their fallen comrades and continued to swarm.

Runners carried the wounded from the battlefield to where the Healers waited, but Healing took time, especially when they had to keep moving the patients as the armies drew closer.

Ada trotted up and down the line, alternating between sending Healing and energy into the Legerdemainian soldiers and lighting strikes into the Ryshaelan. The Ryshaelans across the river had regrouped. They'd found the bridge, and though they could only cross a few at a time, reinforcements were quickly making their way to the battle.

Ada pulled a diamond from her pouch, the biggest one she had. Diamonds were extremely powerful conduits, and using it for what she intended could leave her immobile for some time, but she had to risk it.

She turned her horse back toward the Healers and found Gerdwin. She handed him a topaz and a pouch of herbs. "I'm going to try something. If I am injured in the process, I need you to make me swallow these, and then direct as much Healing energy into me as you can. Do you understand?"

Gerdwin nodded.

Ada dismounted and held the diamond in her hands. Closing her eyes, she drew on every ounce of magic she could grasp and funneled it into the diamond. Then, when it contained as much as it could hold, she formed it into a blast of lightning and directed it at the bridge.

Bodies of men and horses flew into the air as the bridge exploded. Ada watched just long enough to see that the bridge was completely destroyed before collapsing.

She woke to the bitter taste of healing herbs on her tongue. Gerdwin hovered over her.

"Is she all right?" a voice asked.

She turned her head slightly. "Cornan?"

"I'm here," he said.

"You should be fighting."

"I am fighting," he grinned down at her.

Ada held out her hands to the two men. "Help me up."

"You should rest," Cornan said.

"I don't have time to rest. How long was I out?"

"Just a few minutes, my lady," Gerdwin said.

"Good. How's the battle?"

"Better," Cornan said. "The bridge exploding sent the army into a bit of chaos. Enough to drive them back a little."

"We must press the advantage," Ada said. "Where's my horse?"

Gerdwin brought it to her, and she rode toward where the two armies still clashed.

Destroying the bridge was good, but not enough. Already, the Ryshaelans had found a place to ford, picking their way through where the water slowed a mile or so to the east. They'd circle around from that side while the Legerdemainians were still focused and close the trap around them.

Ada beckoned to Beactri and three more of the sorcerers who had fallen to the back of the line, clearly wearied by their efforts. "This way," she said.

With looks of resolve pushing past the exhaustion, they followed her northeast, toward the Sapphire. Cornan came, too.

She stopped when they were parallel with the oncoming soldiers. "We must stop them, any way we can."

She drew more gemstones—rubies and a garnet—out of her pouch and handed them out. "Channel the magic through those—it will help enhance the volatility."

She began sending lightning bolts down toward the enemy, while Cornan went ahead to cut down any who survived the magic.

"Beactri, take a few sorcerers west and cut off any who are trying to ford downstream," Ada instructed.

Beactri nodded and rode back toward the battle.

Two of the three remaining sorcerers followed Ada's lead, sending lightning bolts and other pulses of magical energy at the invaders.

Ada glanced at the third—Elya, if Ada remembered correctly. She had her eyes closed like she was concentrating, but nothing happened. Her lack of participation was an annoying distraction, one Ada could not afford. She tried to remind herself that these people had only learned how to use magic a few days prior, and she couldn't expect too much of them. The girl was trying, and that was all she could ask.

She focused again on the soldiers fording the river. A large swath had broken off of the main force to come this way, and far to the west, another group had found a way across at another ford.

Perhaps she should leave these three here and go join Beactri and the other group on the west side…

No, there wasn't time. She just had to trust that the army and the other sorcerers could handle it and stay focused here.

A soldier made it past the magic that Ada and the others directed their way, barreling toward the main force.

Cornan sliced him down, but another followed. There were too many.

The earth rumbled, and something started to protrude from the ground near the river.

All at once, a tree shot up, right beneath an oncoming soldier, sending him flying from his horse.

Ada whirled around to see the girl who had been concentrating, now with a smile on her face.

"Did you do that?" Ada asked.

Elya nodded.

"How?"

"I… I'm not sure. I just felt the seedling in the ground, and made it bigger."

"Can you do it again?"

The girl nodded. "I think so."

Ada circled on her horse and pressed her hands to the Elya's head as the girl performed the spell again, feeling the magic, the directive that the girl had sent.

"This is good. Do it again, as many times as you can. Create a tree line all along the river, heading east and north. See if we can direct where they can get across to a narrower area so they can't spread out and overwhelm us."

The girl nodded, and a moment later, another tree sprouted, and another.

Ada did the same, and then felt the ground for tangles and underbrush seeds, drawing them in, as well, to create a barrier.

She took the hand of one the others and showed her how to replicate the process, and then the third. In moments, a forest had begun to sprout. The enemy army fell back, trying to find a way around the trees, slowing them down considerably.

Cornan saw what was happening and rode toward the east, catching any who stumbled through the trees.

That was the turning point. Trees springing up created enough confusion to distract the Ryshaelans, whose numbers on the Legerdemainian side were already significantly diminished, giving the Legerdemainians the upper hand to drive them back and cut them down. In a few more moments, it became clear that Legerdemain was in control.

When the Ryshaelans saw what was happening, their leader, directing from across the river, pulled them back, presumably to regroup and develop a new strategy.

Ada led her small group toward King Ondrei.

After they made camp and sent the wounded to the Healers, Ada met with Ondrei and the War Council.

"Send a dove to the sorcerers stationed at the dams," she instructed. "Leave one or two at the each dam to man it, but have the rest come here immediately. We need them to help grow the forest. There are at least a few miles on this side of the river that can be turned into forest. We'll leave the road clear, so we have a trade route after the war is over, but encircle the rest of the kingdom, just inside the river. It will force them to come in through a funnel, which will be much easier to defend."

The king sent the messenger to do her bidding, and the Council began strategizing for the next battle.

There was hope for this war yet.

Spies

"The scouts say the Ryshaelans have made camp beyond the river."
King Ondrei sat in the tent that had been erected for the War Council on
the battlefield. Ada had suggested that they adjourn to the inn in the
South Village, and while he had agreed to sleep there, he wanted the
command tent to be close at hand during the next battle. "They estimate
a solid ten percent were lost today."

"Any idea whether they plan to attack tomorrow?" Ada asked,
pacing the tent.

He gazed at her. She looked so tired, and yet there was a fierceness
in her eyes that revealed her true strength.

"Ondrei," she said again, forcing him back to reality.

"Oh. Er, no idea, as yet. I think the thing with the trees has made
them wary. They're starting to grasp the full scope of our power."

"Good. Let them think we're going easy on them. How many did we
lose today?"

"Not as many as I feared. Several hundred. But many were still alive
and were taken to the Healers."

"Several hundred is still more than we can afford, but I'm glad it
wasn't worse. I'll check in on the Healers in a bit."

"You need to rest," Ondrei said.

"I don't have time to rest. Have the sorcerers come down from the
dams yet?"

"We only sent the dove a few hours ago. Even if they have gotten
ready, they wouldn't leave until morning. Ada."

She stopped her pacing to look at him.

"You need to rest. I can't afford for you to be exhausted."

"What if something happens while I'm resting? What if we lose this
war so I can take a nap?"

"That's why we have scouts and guards on duty. They will alert us. Please. Come with me to the inn and let's get some sleep." He held out his hand to her, and for once, she took it.

She must be truly exhausted. Usually she kept her distance—the boundaries between them firmly erected.

Her hand nestled into his, warm and delicate and soft. He'd known her his whole life, and she never seemed to change. She was the one constant in everything. She'd comforted him when his father died and helped him transition into his role as king. She'd taught him everything he knew, and helped him to be a good king—a good man.

She had to be considerably older than he was, and yet she never seemed to age. She was still the most beautiful woman he'd ever seen.

Signaling his guards to accompany them, he helped Ada onto her horse, mounted his, and led the way to the South Village.

The inn stood empty, evacuated like everything else, but the door was not barred, so Ondrei led the way inside and helped himself to the dried meat and fruit in the pantry, sharing some with Ada and with the guards.

Ada nibbled at the food he'd set in front of her, still clearly distracted.

He sighed. "Set a watch," he said to his guards. "Alert us if anything happens or if anyone comes."

He took Ada by the hand and led her upstairs to one of the rooms.

"You worked yourself too hard today."

"I didn't work any harder than you or anyone else."

"But you did. You directed everyone and kept them from losing heart. And you used some very powerful spells, which I know drained your energy."

He sat next to her on one of the beds and put a hand on her shoulder. "It's not over yet. I need you to stay strong."

He lightly rubbed her shoulder with his fingertips and almost immediately felt her begin to relax. Shifting slightly, he positioned himself behind her so he could massage both shoulders.

The tension in them diminished a bit, and her head started to nod, so he gently laid her down on the bed and pulled the blanket up over her.

She was asleep almost immediately.

Ondrei stared at her for a short while before returning downstairs.

He had fought hard that day, as well, but he could not yet rest. He was expecting a visitor any moment.

Sure enough, a few minutes later, the door to the inn opened and one of the soldiers stuck his head in. "There's someone here to see you," he said.

"Let him in," Ondrei said.

A cloaked figure pushed past the guard and flopped down at the table, helping himself to the dried meat and fruit that still sat there.

Ondrei waited until the soldier closed the door. "Well?"

His guest pushed back his hood, revealing the swarthy features of his Oajuran ancestry and stuffed a dried apple chunk into his mouth. "The camp is in an uproar."

"That's as we suspected. How did you get across the river?"

"Shot an arrow with a rope attached into a tree. That's… spectacular. I haven't seen that many trees since I left the coast. Anyway, I held on to the rope and swam across. Fine for one person, but not practical for a whole army."

"What are they discussing in their War Council?"

"The king is recruiting assassins whose sole purpose it will be to get through the front lines and attack the sorcerers. But there's also a rumor that he's consulting with his advisors about getting sorcerers of their own."

"Like you?"

The man shrugged. "My people were all but wiped out in the war. That's why I came here in the first place. I have no desire to be enslaved to Ryshael. And my suspicion is that none others do, either. Most of us fled across the sea or were killed, so I doubt he'll find too many willing to help him."

"Even one is too many. We're being slaughtered as it is. You're sure they don't have a sorcerer among them?"

"I'm absolutely certain."

"Good. Then go back to your post."

"There's one more thing."

Ondrei raised an eyebrow and waited for him to continue.

"There's a spy somewhere in your midst. They haven't heard an update in several days. They were waiting for word, which is why they waited so long to attack. They finally decided the spy must be dead or incapacitated and attacked anyway, but there's still a chance the spy is just waiting for the right time. Be careful what you say, and to whom."

Ondrei nodded. "Thank you. Watch out for patrols. They're guarding the forest carefully to make sure no one gets through."

"Don't worry about me," the Oajuran grinned.

A puff of greenish gray smoke filled the air, and when it dissipated, the man was gone. It would've been quite impressive if Ondrei hadn't heard the squeak of hinges coming from the door to the kitchen. Still, though, even a minimally talented sorcerer like that one had his uses.

But now Ondrei had a spy to worry about, in addition to everything else.

He made his way upstairs and lay next to Ada on the bed, sleep coming to him at last.

Turncoat

The door slammed open with a heavy thud, pulling Ada from a restless sleep.

She looked up to see Cornan standing in the doorway, his face pale. His gaze landed on her waist. She glanced down to see Ondrei's arm draped over her. Annoyed, she shoved it away and sat up.

"What is it?" she asked.

Cornan's eyes shifted to her face.

"Ryshaelans. On foot, coming by the thousands through the trees."

"How did they cross the river?"

"Ropes. They created a pulley system using our own trees to loop the ropes around so the soldiers can climb hand-over-hand across the river. Hundreds of them, all along the bank."

Ondrei stirred and sat up. "What's going on?"

"Ryshaelans. Using ropes to cross the river. Coming through the forest on foot," Ada said.

Ondrei's face darkened.

"On foot is better than horseback," Ada said. "Line up the army along the forest and cut them down as soon as they come through."

"We've already begun, my lady," Cornan said.

Ada winced. He sounded so formal, so… distant. Completely opposite the friendly camaraderie they'd begun to develop. Curse Ondrei and his too-familiar hands.

She leapt from the bed. "Any news on the sorcerers coming down from the mountains?"

"Received a dove this morning. They are on their way. Should be here by afternoon."

"I just hope we last that long. Gather all the sorcerers and have them meet me by the Healers. We need to discuss a strategy."

Cornan bowed and hurried away.

Ada turned to glare at Ondrei, preparing to give him a tongue-lashing for his inappropriateness, but stopped herself. Now was not the time. They had work to do. She stomped from the room and down the stairs.

Outside, the king's guard waited, at the ready.

She pointed to one. "You, get my horse. You will accompany me to the battlefield. The rest of you, wait for the king. He'll be along shortly."

Cornan stood nearby, standing straight, rigid and formal.

"You should come, too," Ada told him. "We're going to need everyone with magical abilities."

He nodded, but still did not acknowledge her as more than a fellow soldier. She sighed, hating that it bothered her so.

The sorcerers were already assembled when Ada arrived.

"The trees have forced the Ryshaelans to adopt a new tactic. They're now coming in on foot, which slows them down, but there are still far too many of them. Our soldiers are cutting them down as they come through the forest, but it's only a matter of time until we can't keep up. They have adapted, and so must we. I need three groups. Beactri, you will lead the first group. Go join the soldiers at the front and kill as many soldiers as they emerge from the trees as possible."

Beactri nodded.

Ada continued. "The second will continue building the forest. Eventually they'll make their way to the northwestern or northeastern ends of the forest and just go around, so the further they have to travel, the better. Also, the more trees they have to fight through to get to us, the more tired they'll be and easier to defeat. The forest is still our best defense, so let's continue working on that."

She paused before speaking again. "The third group will be performing by far the most dangerous task. I will not assign anyone to this duty, but anyone who wishes to volunteer would be appreciated. This group will need to make their way through the forest, past the enemy. You'll need to get close to the river and start cutting down their lines so they can't get across."

"I'll go," Cornan said immediately.

Ada's jaw clenched. She should've assumed he'd be the first to volunteer. Foolish, beautiful, brave man. She nodded, however. "Thank you. Anyone else?"

A few more shuffled over to stand next to Cornan.

"Very good. The rest of you, do you have a preference whether you'd prefer to be on forest duty or army duty?"

The group divided fairly evenly, even without her prompting.

Ada nodded to the group who would be joining the army. "Intersperse yourselves as evenly as you can." She turned to the forest group. "Half of you go east, and half west, and work on both extending the treeline along the river heading north, and expanding the width of the forest. The rest of you, come with me. We'll start as far north as possible and make our way down the bank toward where the army is coming through."

"You're not coming," Cornan said.

Ada rolled her eyes. "This is the most important job. Of course I'm coming."

"You're needed here. What if something happens to you?"

"Something could happen to me just as easily here as there. I need to see their army for myself in order to come up with a plan. Let's go."

The two other groups dispersed, all except for one young woman.

The girl who had started the forest with that first tree. Elya.

"My lady… might I have a word first?" she asked, her voice timid and her hands trembling.

"Of course," Ada said. She turned to Cornan. "Go on ahead. I'll join you shortly."

She turned back to Elya. "What is it?"

"There's something you should know. I… I am not Legerdemanian."

Ada narrowed her eyes. "What do you mean?"

"I was sent as a spy from Ryshael. I was supposed to report back the movements of the army and your defense systems, and I did, for awhile."

She gulped and Ada reached out a hand and placed it on her arm. "It's all right. You can tell me."

Elya nodded. "I took a job as a merchant's apprentice. I told him I was from the North Village, so he wouldn't wonder where I came from, and so I had access to his gossip. I took reports every few days to my contact on the other side of the river. I told him…" she choked again. "I told him of your plan to recruit and train people in magic use. And… and he sent the assassin. I'm so sorry! I didn't know, I was just…"

She broke off, sobs wracking her body.

Ada placed a hand on the girl's head and felt deep inside her mind, feeling the weight of truth that lay there. "Elya. It all worked out. But... why are you telling me this now?"

"Because I don't want to be Ryshaelan. I want to be Legerdemaninan. I want to help you. I was there, in the square, when you were training. I didn't mean to, but I started following your directions, and then... I could feel it! I didn't know I could use magic, but I can, and I... I don't want to go back. I want to go with you to the river, but if they see me..."

Ada took the girl's hands. She smiled. "I believe you. And I have a very important job for you, if you think you can do it."

Elya nodded. "Anything, my lady."

Supplies

Elya moved through the trees—*her* trees. She could still feel them, feel her connection to them through the magic she'd used to create them. Not that she'd actually created anything—she'd only used what was already there and encouraged its growth.

Still, the feeling of ownership and accomplishment covered her like a warm blanket. She'd built this forest. Using magic. The same magic her uncle claimed was evil. But he was wrong. He didn't want to create or build or enjoy, only to control.

He was as bad as the gods he claimed to serve, seeking to destroy so that he held the power.

King Ondrei wasn't like that. He didn't want to conquer or rule. He was more a governor than dictator, leading the people when necessary, enforcing and upholding the law, but never encroaching on his people's freedom. The people lived and worked and traded and were free to come and go and do as they pleased.

Even in this war, the people were asked to join the army or the sorcerers, not forced. There was no demand, only a plea. The thousands and thousands of Ryshaelan troops invading Legerdemain did so at the demand of the king, with the threat of losing their homes, families, and livelihoods if they did not comply.

King Ondrei was a good king, and Legerdemain was a good country.

And now she had a chance to do something to save it.

She made it to the edge of the river. Already, Ada and her sorcerers were several hundred feet down the bank, slicing through the ropes with magic, sending Ryshaelan troops into the water.

Those who made it across didn't stop to fight the sorcerers, but pushed on through the trees to join the main battle.

Smart. Her uncle must have instructed them to overwhelm the army and go straight for the king rather than try to fight the sorcerers one-on-one. Although he would surely have people—archers or assassins—preparing to target the sorcerers and rid them of their magical strategy. But mostly he was relying on sheer manpower to overtake Legerdemain. And he would win, eventually.

Unless this plan worked.

Elya went upstream a little, then summoned magic and used it to hold several branches—broken from her trees as the army tromped through the newly made forest—together, into a sort of bridge. It was weak, and the magic would dissipate quickly, but it would hold long enough for her to get across.

Even in the few days she'd been practicing magic, she had begun to trust her own abilities and the spells she wove together.

She ran across her little bridge and jumped to the opposite bank.

Several horses grazed on the lush grass at the bank of the river, left by the soldiers who had gone across by rope. She mounted one and raced toward the Ryshaelan camp.

Her uncle's tent was guarded by several men—that meant he was still in there. Unlike King Ondrei, who led the charge to protect his country. A flash of disgust shot through her at her uncle's selfishness.

She dismounted and rushed into the tent. The guards didn't even try to stop her—they must have had instructions to let her in whenever she arrived.

Her uncle looked up from a table covered with maps and papers when she entered. "Where have you been?" he demanded.

"They evacuated the town where I was staying, and I had to go along or risk being uncovered. I could not get away until now."

"It's a little late. You didn't tell me what their plans were with the rivers or the sorcerers. You said she was training—you didn't tell me there were hundreds of them!"

Elya fought to keep from rolling her eyes. There weren't hundreds—a few dozen, at best. But part of her plan relied on him thinking they were stronger than they were. "I didn't know their plans with the rivers. I'm not in the king's inner circle. I've told you all I can. But that's why I came. They're planning something, something big."

Her uncle straightened. "What do you mean?"

"They're building some sort of weapon, something powered by magic."

"I have seen no construction whatsoever."

"There's a farmhouse along the west side of the country. So average you'd never notice it, outside the bounds of the West Village. But there's a barn. They're building it inside the barn."

"What is it?"

Elya shook her head. "I don't know. I just know that at least half the sorcerers and many of the soldiers are not on the front lines because they're working on the weapon. Uncle, I... I fear they may be able to overpower us with this."

He sneered at her. "You don't even know what it is."

"Yes, but I have seen the power of their magic up close. Pull our people out. Leave this country behind, I beg you, or they'll kill us all."

"They cannot win. And they cannot hope that anything they build will prevail against our numbers. Already, we are overcoming them. I'll send men to this farmhouse to sabotage whatever it is they're building."

"You cannot sabotage magic, Majesty."

"We shall see."

Elya gave an exaggerated sigh. "Don't say I didn't warn you. I should get back. I'm supposed to be helping tend the wounded. I need to go before I am missed and they start asking questions."

She left the tent and mounted her horse. She rode out, back toward the direction she'd come, in case anyone was watching. Then, once she was out of sight, she circled back around and made her way to the Ryshaelan supply tents and found the supply master.

"Greetings, Highness," he said with a bow.

"I have been sent by my uncle on a sensitive mission. I need half a dozen hands to help me take supplies across the river. Our troops are being overrun."

"How is that possible?" the supply master asked.

"They are using their magic. They are more powerful than we could have imagined, and they will destroy us all. But my uncle will not listen to reason. He has taken this war as a personal affront, and he will not rest until all our people are dead. Legerdemain is not what we thought. They are free and peaceful. They want nothing more than to be allowed to live their lives. None of their soldiers are conscripted—they are all fighting of their own free will to save their way of life. There is no way we can win against that."

"Surely their magic will consume them and the gods will destroy them," the supply master said, his voice choked.

"Will they? I have seen no evidence that the gods actually care. I have only seen a people who love their country and will do whatever it takes to defend it."

She smiled to herself. The supply master would spread those thoughts to everyone who came near, and very soon discontent would infect the entire army. And fear. The superstition of her people demanded fear of the gods. But if the gods weren't on their side, or didn't care…

She led twelve stable hands and twelve carts full of food and weapons away from the supply tent. It wasn't much, but every little bit that she could take from Ryshael and give to Legerdemain would help.

She stopped them at the bank of the river, near her little bridge. "The river is enchanted. It is not safe for all of us to cross. As the king's niece, it is my duty to see this mission through. I will not risk your lives. Return tonight at dusk to this spot, with another cart each, and I will take them across and deliver them to our troops… If I survive."

Weapon

Ada turned as Elya came toward her, towing twelve carts of supplies behind her, roped together with magic and pulled by one horse. She laughed. That girl was a genius.

"Brilliant," she said, waving at the carts.

Elya blushed deeply under her olive skin. "Thank you, my lady."

"What news do you have? Did it work?"

Elya nodded. "My uncle is more determined than ever to destroy this country. He believes sheer numbers will eventually overtake you."

Ada nodded. "And they will. If we don't stop them first. The plan?"

"It's working. He believes we are building a huge weapon in a barn near the West Village. He is sending men to sabotage it."

"Perfect. We'll be waiting for them."

"My lady…" Elya paused. "What is the plan? If we aren't really building a weapon, what will we do with them?"

"Nothing. I will set up magical traps to hold them hostage. We'll keep them prisoner. We won't kill them, but neither will they be able to do any harm."

"Won't that be pointless, in the long run?" Elya asked. "My uncle will only send more, but it won't be enough to affect the overall numbers of the army."

Ada sighed. How much should she tell this girl? She was a defector, yes, but how much loyalty did she still hold for her people, and especially her uncle, the king? "To be honest, I'm not entirely sure. I am trying everything I can think of to win this war, and every little piece, no matter how small, will help. If your uncle's trusted spies disappear without a word, it will cause him to be anxious. Perhaps anxious enough to make a mistake."

That was the best she could do. Even if Elya returned to her own people, she wouldn't know the full extent of what Ada had prepared.

Ada left Elya to distribute the supplies she'd brought, and raced toward Ondrei's war council tent.

Ondrei was inside, resting from the long battle he'd fought that morning. His magical protection had save him, but he'd been injured being knocked from his horse, and the Healers were attending to him.

"Leave us," Ondrei said to the Healers when she entered.

Ada waited until they were alone to speak. "It worked. The Ryshaelan king believes we're building a weapon. He is sending his men to sabotage it."

"And what are we really doing?" Ondrei winced as he tried to move toward her.

"I have a spell in place that will trap them, and another that will cause them to see visions. They already have it in their minds that we're constructing a great weapon, so it will become whatever their minds choose to see. They will believe, with everything in their being, that we have created a weapon so devastating that they will not be able to survive. They will be afraid—so very afraid—that they will likely defect, and if we're very lucky, they will convince others to, as well."

"And if we're not lucky?"

"It will buy us time to come up with another plan."

Ada left his tent. She had to go to the West Village and implement her traps. The spells were so delicate, so precise, she could not trust them to anyone else. But she did need backup. She beckoned to two of the Healers and a handful of soldiers. "Come with me," she said.

She found a suitable farm near the West Village, and turned to the soldiers. "I need four of you to set up a perimeter around that barn. Guard it as if the king himself is taking refuge therein. Set up watches and patrols, and let no one through."

She led the rest of them into the barn. "When I am done here, none of you will be allowed in without being accompanied by me. I am expecting spies from Ryshael to come to this location, and when they do, they will be trapped in here for a period of time. When they escape—and they will escape—allow them to go. They will tell their king stories of great horrors they witnessed here."

She showed the Healers an assortment of herbs. "I need you to go to the river and find as many of these as you can. They should be growing in abundance along the bank of the river, even in this weather."

The left and she addressed the soldiers. "When the Ryshaelan spies escape, they need to believe, absolutely, that it was their own ingenuity that did it. Put up a fight. Make sure you preserve your own lives, but don't let them leave easily. I want you to guard the doors and windows. And whatever you do, don't come in. The spells I will be placing on this room will be as powerful against you as they are against the enemy."

The soldiers nodded their understanding.

"Good. Now, gather wagons, carts, farming equipment—anything you can find, and stack it in the center of the room."

They obeyed, and in a short time, had built a tower of random machinery and furniture. Ada dusted the entire structure with a potion, then placed gemstones, mostly rubies, on boards and shelves along various points. She then wove an intricate web of magic that would send shocks through anyone who touched it, activating the place in their minds that controlled fear.

Just looking at it would cause panic and nausea, but one touch and they would be nearly catatonic with fright. They would scarcely be able to describe what they saw, but it would leave them trembling.

When that was done, she took a step back and wove another spell on top of it, a mirage that made the entire structure seem to shimmer and glow.

The soldiers still with her gasped.

"What... what is it?" one of them asked.

"It's an illusion. It is whatever your mind wants it to be. The herbs that the Healers are bringing back will be made into a potion that I will use to cover the outside of the barn. That potion will control the minds of anyone who touches it and cause them to believe whatever they are told. In this case, they have been informed that inside this barn is a weapon of great power. So when they look through a window or crack in the walls, that is what they will see."

"If only we really could build a weapon like that," he sighed.

"We have a weapon like that. His name is King Ondrei. He just doesn't know it yet."

Dissention

"You were right."

Elya's eyes widened. Her uncle had never said such a thing before. Not even close. Especially ironic, since she was lying.

"I sent six men to sabotage the weapon. Only three returned, and they only barely with their lives."

"The weapon is…" Elya choked back her words. She'd almost said "real." She took a deep breath to steady her words. "The weapon is that powerful?"

Her uncle nodded. "It was huge, and glowing with power. So large that it is nearly indescribable. All three had slightly different interpretations of what they saw, but they could all feel the evil magic pulsing from it. It made them ill. And who knows what it did to the others. The three who are missing touched it, and fell over, probably killed instantly. The three who escaped had to fight guards and sorceresses to get out. We have to destroy it."

"How?" Elya asked. "If it kills anyone who touches it…"

"We must find a way to destroy it without touching it. I need you."

"Of course, Majesty. You know I will do whatever I can to help win his war."

"Good girl. You have been working with the Healers, yes?"

Elya nodded.

"Healers are sorcerers."

"Yes," Elya said.

"I want you to talk to them. They should trust you enough by now to confide in you. Find out how the weapon works, and if it has any weaknesses."

"Majesty, I will try… but even if I find that out, it is magic. I know nothing of magic or how to stop it."

Her uncle slammed his hand down on the table, sending papers flying. "By the gods, Elya, I don't have time for you to be a coward like your father. You must do this. Do you understand? You *must*. If we lose this war, I will hold you personally responsible."

Rage swelled within her. She was no coward. But let him believe she was. It was almost time to show him where the power truly lay.

"I will discover how to destroy it, if such a thing is possible," she said.

"If you can, spread rumors about us gathering more troops. I need to regroup and get my army motivated, and I can't do that with this threat of a weapon hanging over them. It needs to be destroyed. When it is, we will overwhelm them and leave none of them alive to plan revenge or insurrection. Especially the magic-wielding abominations. Get going. I will not lose this war. Do you understand?"

She nodded and scurried from the tent.

He was withdrawing his army. Temporarily, to be sure, but such a reprieve would be enough to rally Legerdemain. She couldn't wait to tell Ada.

She had one thing left to do, however.

She made her way to the food tents. Some of the cooks knew her and smiled.

"Elya," one man grinned. She couldn't remember his name, but his son had tried to court her once upon a time.

"Good morning," she smiled. "What is that? It smells delicious."

"Mutton stew," he smiled.

She inhaled deeply. "I've missed our food. Legerdemain has some strange recipes."

"Ah, but you're doing important work, I hear. How soon do you expect we'll win this war?"

Elya looked around, as though to make sure no one was listening. "I confess, I don't have much hope for that. You have heard about the weapon?"

The cook's face paled and he nodded slowly.

"My uncle wants me to find a way to destroy it, but I fear it is hopeless. It cannot be destroyed. It is magical, and it kills anyone who touches it. They are too powerful. They will destroy us if we go back across their borders."

She glanced over her shoulder again, then leaned close. "You mustn't tell anyone I said so, but were the king not my uncle, I would defect. Run away to Kirland or Sunnland or somewhere far away and never return. Legerdemain would leave us in peace if we give up this fight, but they will not be conquered."

The cook gulped. "Well, you must find a way to destroy that weapon, then."

She nodded. "I'll try."

He gave her a bowl of soup and a chunk of bread, and she wished him well before she walked away. She told the same story a few more times, to cooks, stable hands, and even a few of the soldiers who stopped her to talk.

Legerdemain was small, and their king was kind. They did not understand that ruling a country the size of Ryshael and forcing them into a war involved a great deal of strong-armed dictatorship and threats. As long as they believed they would be victorious, and then richly rewarded, the people would comply. But fighting a war they could not win? Giving up their lives for the king's pointless ambition?

The seeds of dissent were already there, and she'd just helped them to sprout, like she'd done with the trees in the field.

She would bet by the time her uncle made a plan to move forward again, a solid third of the army would have defected.

She mounted her horse and made her way back to Legerdemain.

"Where is Ada?" she asked the Healers when she returned.

"In the War Council tent," Gerdwin said.

She hurried over. Her news could not wait.

The guard at the door let her in.

King Ondrei, Ada, and a few members of the War Council sat around the table, talking.

Ada smiled when she entered. "Elya, come in. Your Majesty, may I introduce our spy?"

Elya gave an awkward curtsy.

"How did it go?" Ada asked.

"My… King Jando wants me to find out if the weapon has any weaknesses and how to destroy it. He is withdrawing his troops to regroup until I can find out how to destroy the weapon, and then he'll attack again."

"Good. That buys us some time," Ada said. "What else?"

"I have spread rumors among the soldiers and workers that the weapon will kill us all. I expect mass defection from the army over the next few days."

96

"Excellent. With luck, by the time they figure out that the weapon is non-existent, we will have our defenses renewed. Well done, Elya."

The king stared at her, appraising. "You accomplished all that?"

Her face felt hot, and she lowered her eyes. "Yes, Majesty."

"No need to be so formal, here. You may call me King Ondrei. I am in your debt, Elya. Thank you."

"It is my pleasure, Your… King Ondrei." She curtsied again and hurried out of the tent, stopping when she got to the Healers' tent to finally breathe.

King Ondrei himself called her by name and thanked her. He said she could call him by his name. How could anyone serve a man like her uncle when there were kings like King Ondrei in the world?

Proposal

"Ada, may I have a word?"

"Of course, Your Majesty."

King Ondrei waited until the last of his advisors filed from the war council tent before taking Ada's hand. "This battle would be lost—*I'd be lost* without you."

She smiled but pulled her hand away. "I know."

He faltered. He'd intended to go on when she protested, as he was sure she would, about how much he wanted her by his side. Her matter-of-fact acceptance of his words left him somewhat at a loss.

He reached for her hand again, but she placed it firmly in her lap, away from his reach.

He pressed on anyway. "It's not just as an advisor that I appreciate you. I also enjoy you as a companion and I desire you… as a woman."

She laughed.

The sound was musical, filling the air. He couldn't help but be drawn to the sound, despite that she was laughing at him.

"You are aware that I'm old enough to be your great grandmother?"

"You don't look it."

She arched an eyebrow. "Do not be fooled by my shell, Majesty. Over a hundred years of life have changed me more than you can imagine. I'm not a maiden to be wooed."

"Yes, but it is exactly that wisdom and experience that I admire so."

Ada stood and stepped away from the table, crossing her arms in front of her chest. "I delivered you from your mother's womb and disciplined you for your naughtiness more than once. I still see you as the child I helped raise."

Ondrei stiffened. He had to fight to keep the irritation from his voice when he answered her. "As you can well see, I am no longer a boy. I am a man, a king."

"Yes, and a fine one. You lead your people with wisdom and compassion."

"Then why will you not accept my affections? You admit I have become a fine man. This kingdom would benefit immensely from you as its queen. And I... nothing would make me happier. After we win this war—"

"Thank you, Majesty, but no."

Ondrei clenched his jaw. Her continued refusal was starting to grate on him. "What about your duty to this kingdom?"

Ada's eyes narrowed. "I have served this kingdom faithfully through many kings before you, and I will continue to serve it for many more after you are dead and gone."

Ondrei lifted his hands, as if in surrender. "I have no heir. If we lose this war there will be no one to carry on my line. But you and I together—we could preserve the royal line. Our children would be powerful. Me, a king, and you a sorceress."

"If we lose this war, there will be no kingdom to carry on, and if we win, you will have plenty of time to woo and wed after."

"I wish to woo *you*, Ada. None other. And I can't imagine that you don't also have feelings for me, after all we've been through together. Why will you not even consider it? Surely it must be lonely, all these years with no companion."

"I knew when I accepted the charge of guardian of this realm that love would never be part of my life. My legacy is this land. I shall never marry, never have babies."

Ondrei clenched a fist. He hadn't expected her to be so stubborn. But he *would* marry her, one way or another. "You will if I order it. I am your king. You serve me and you will obey me."

Ada stood. Her eyes, which were usually warm pools, turned to stone. "Do you think you're the first king to ever propose to me? Ever to claim to love me? You are a foolish child, to think you know anything about me, about the role I play in this kingdom. You will never know fully what I do to protect this land and its rulers, and you will never know how much that duty has cost me."

A rustled at the tent flap interrupted any further discussion. "Enter," Ondrei said.

One of the soldiers, a man named Cornan, entered and bowed, but Ondrei didn't miss the way his eyes traveled over Ada before dropping to the floor. "Your Majesty, there is an emissary from King Jando requesting an audience."

"Prepare my guards in my tent. I'll receive him shortly."

"Yes, Your Majesty."

The soldier left, but Ada continued to stare at the door for a long moment. "Jando will not want to negotiate," she said without turning. "He is certain of his victory. Anything he offers you will be a trap."

"What do you suggest I do?"

"Play along." She turned to face him at last, her expression impassive. "Ask questions about what sort of treaty he's willing to pursue. Keep him talking. I will see what I can glean from his words—if I can sense any hint of the state of their army or their resources."

"What should I say?"

"Bluff. He knows we know he's stronger than we are, but he fears our weapon. He is stalling until he can dismantle it, which means he believes he will soon have us at his mercy. Pretend you're willing to negotiate. Most people give away more than they realize, both when they think they're winning, and when they know they're losing. I should be able to figure out what he has planned if you keep him talking long enough."

"Very well." Ondrei stood and offered her his arm.

She took it, but kept her body rigid, her posture distant and cold as he led the way to the throne room.

He sighed. "You are certain you'll never marry?"

Ada didn't look at him when she answered. "As I said, I knew from the beginning love would never be a part of my life."

He nodded, feigning acquiescence for the moment. But her decision was far from final. He would see to it.

Negotiations

Elya sat in a chair behind a curtain in the king's tent. Ada had invited her to listen to the negotiations, and offer insight into what her uncle might be planning.

Ada stood behind Ondrei as he sat in the wooden chair that had been brought to serve as a throne. Ondrei sat upright and fiddled with the amulet around his neck. Ada placed a hand on his head. Elya could feel the calm energy Ada directed into him. It would not do for him to be seen as nervous or weak.

Ada glanced at her.

Elya nodded, indicating she was ready.

Ada turned and nodded to the guard who stood by the front entrance. "You may let him in."

The flap opened and three men walked in, one dressed in the finery of a lord, flanked by two soldiers. Elya peeked through a tiny slit in the curtain. Broden. Of course her uncle would've sent him. That pompous ass had designs on power, even to the point of trying to convince Jando to let him marry Elya. Another good reason to have defected to Legerdemain. But she kept her face impassive. She didn't want to distract Ada from the task at hand.

The emissary bowed. "Greetings, King Ondrei. I am Lord Broden, emissary of King Jando of Ryshael. I have come to discuss the terms of your surrender."

Ondrei coughed on a laugh. "Is that what you think?"

"You cannot overpower us," Lord Broden said. "We will pick away at your army, little by little, until you are entirely overcome. Your people, innocents—farmers, craftsmen, merchants, children—will all be destroyed. This land will be absorbed into Ryshael, one way or another.

However, King Jando is lenient. He is willing to allow you to surrender and save the lives of your people."

Elya clenched her jaw. Jando knew exactly the right tack to take.

Ada glanced surreptitiously at her.

Elya shook her head. *Lies*, she mouthed silently.

Ada pressed her hand against Ondrei's shoulder to communicate to him not to believe the emissary.

Ondrei laughed again. "You expect me to believe that? Your words are the pleas of a desperate man. You would slaughter us all even if we surrendered. You know we are now in a position to defeat you, and so you think by this show of bravado to make us cower? My scouts say soldiers are defecting from your armies by the hundreds."

"A ploy we have allowed you to believe," Lord Broden smiled. "In reality, they are recruiting more soldiers to our cause. In a few days' time, we will have twice the number we started with. Your weapon will not overpower so many. We will destroy it, and you with it, unless you surrender peacefully now."

So they still believed the weapon was functional. That was good.

"Let's assume, for the moment, that anything you say is believable. What would the terms of surrender be?"

"Legerdemain would become a vassal state under Ryshael, subject to any and all laws and taxes therein, but your citizens would be allowed to continue living and working here, and a representative of your own people would be set to govern and report to Ryshael. One thing would not be negotiable, however. Magic use will be outlawed, and any known magic users will be sent to Ryshael for trial and punishment under Ryshaelan law."

"Absolutely not. I am not subjecting half my population to death under Ryshael's arcane anti-magic laws."

"Then prepare to be invaded. If you reject this offer, we will show no mercy."

"You try my patience," Ondrei said. "There is nothing preventing us from crossing the river and destroying you all. The only reason we haven't is because we believe all life is sacred, even the lives of power-hungry scum like yourselves. We will defend ourselves, whatever that takes. But if you continue to threaten us, we will be forced to change our tactics from defensive to offensive. I assure you, once we cross that river, all is lost for Ryshael."

"We shall see," Lord Broden said. "I will communicate your answer to my king, though I already know his response. You have two days to reconsider, and then you will be destroyed."

He and his guards swept from the room as if it was their own.

King Ondrei sighed. "Well?" he asked.

Ada beckoned to Elya to come out of hiding.

Elya stood before the king and curtsied. "He is lying. Stalling for time, as Ada said. He will not spare anyone. I have no doubt that he is sending more spies to the barn in an attempt to dismantle the weapon."

"So that gives us two days to come up with an actual weapon," he said.

"I cannot just create something out of thin air," Ada snapped. "That's not how it works. I can take energies that already exist and enhance them or point them in a certain direction, but I can't just make a magical weapon that will destroy all our enemies."

"Then what good is magic at all? Why don't we just surrender and let him have Legerdemain? Better half of our people alive without magic than all of us dead despite it."

Elya's heart ached at the choice he faced. How could he be expected to make it? Especially when the treaty was a lie, and they would all die anyway?

Better to die fighting than live as slaves or be slaughtered.

She took a step closer to the king. "My uncle will not be moved. This has become a point of honor with him now. He is incapable of accepting defeat. Even if we had a weapon and could transport it to the river, he would not give up. He will not relent until one of us or the other is utterly destroyed."

"What do we do?" King Ondrei asked.

"We destroy him," Ada said. She turned to Elya. "I hate to ask, because you have already done so much, but we must press our advantage while we can. Can you take some of the other sorcerers into the Ryshaelan camp? We need to sabotage them any way we can. Show them how to avoid the patrols, where the supply tents are—anything that will help us."

Elya nodded. "Pick a team for me of the most skilled but also the most stealthy. The patrols will let me in, but they'll be watching to see if I am followed. I will do what I can to clear the way, but I will need them to be cunning."

"I'll have them meet you in the forest at dusk," Ada said. "Get some rest. We have two days to destroy their army before they attack, and when they do they'll discover that our weapon is nothing but an illusion."

King Ondrei took Elya's hand. Warmth flooded through her as he held on and looked into her eyes. "Thank you."

Elya's heart stuttered and she fought to find the right words. "I… it is my greatest pleasure to serve you, Your Majesty."

Love

"You're doing well with shielding, but you keep shying away from using magic to attack," Ada said. "Try again."

Ondrei stood in the field near the barn where the non-existent weapon sat, trying to practice magic and learn new, more powerful spells to defeat Ryshael.

He lifted his hands and pulled the magic into himself, but as soon as he tried to make it into a lightning bolt, the way Ada did, it fizzled and died. He sighed. "It just feels... different, somehow. Wrong, in a way. You say magic is a tool, and I can accept using the tool to help my people—to Heal and defend—but I have a harder time accepting that I must use it to kill and destroy."

"You use your sword to kill."

"But that's what it was made for. Its entire purpose is to be a weapon. Magic..." He paused, searching for the right words. "The entire continent has outlawed the use of magic because those who used magic grasped only for power and used it to control and dominate their people. If I use magic in the same way, I am no different than those who set themselves up as gods. If I do not use magic correctly, then I do not deserve to use it at all."

Ada touched his arm. He inhaled to keep his breath steady. She was usually so distant. She knew how he felt about her—he could hardly contain his love, despite how harshly she'd turned down his proposal—and so she usually kept her distance. But now she drew closer, so close he could've kissed her if he dared.

But he didn't.

"Ondrei," she said, her voice soft and warm, "the fact that you are so concerned about using magic for good only proves that you are exactly the right person to wield it. These are your people. They are depending on you to save them. Using magic to protect those who cannot protect themselves is not the same as grabbing power for yourself or using it for your own gain. This is a war, and innocent people—*your* people—will die if you do not learn to embrace magic for all it is."

He closed his eyes to keep from getting lost in hers. He almost preferred when she kept her distance.

Almost.

"Think of everyone else who is fighting for Legerdemain." Her voice was pleading now. "How many soldiers have already died? How many sorcerers have sacrificed what they wanted because you won't? What about Elya, who risks herself every time she crosses the river to help us gain information and to sabotage her uncle?"

Elya. The spy. Warmth flooded him at the thought of her. She was so brave. In some ways she reminded him of Ada—both beautiful and strong and powerful and determined...

Ada was right, of course. She always was. Elya and so many others were fighting for him. For Legerdemain. It might not be perfect, but it was good, this country. The freedom to *be* was more powerful than anything those other countries had to offer in their constant quests for more.

"Try again," Ada said. "Use the amulet. Channel the magic through it to create your spell. Remember who you're fighting for. Do it for them."

Ondrei stepped back away from Ada's distracting touch. He focused only on the magic around him, pulling it into himself.

Elya had used magic as both a weapon for defense and a catalyst for the future when she'd made the trees grow. How had she done that? Maybe if he could figure that out, or something similar, he would not feel so guilty about annihilating their enemies. How could he use magic for good while still protecting his people?

He pictured Elya in his mind and imagined her creating a forest. In his mind, he saw her standing there in the field, her dark hair blowing in the wind, her hands glowing with magic, trees and flowers blossoming around her.

"Ondrei," Ada whispered. "How are you doing that?"

He opened his eyes to see what she was talking about.

In the field before them stood an army—but not just an ordinary army. An army of Elya. At least a dozen of her, standing in the field, glowing hands above their heads, while flowers sprang up and waved in the chill air.

"Can you… can you control them?" Ada asked.

"I… I don't know," Ondrei said. "I'm not even sure what I'm doing or how. I was just trying to create instead of destroy."

"Try," Ada said. "Send energy through them and see if you can make them… I don't know, lift a rock or something."

Ondrei felt each of the apparitions through the magic flowing through the amulet. He connected it to the field and found a stone for each of them, then, in unison, they all raised their glowing hands in the air, and with it, rocks floated up around them.

Ada laughed, her voice like chimes.

Ondrei turned to look at her and the army of Elyas faded.

He took a step toward her, not caring that she'd already turned him down, and slid an arm around her waist, pulling her close and resting his forehead against hers. "Ada, the only reason I can do anything is because of you. Why won't you let me love you? Why can't you even consider loving me in return?"

She closed her eyes, her body losing its rigid stance as she leaned into him. "Oh, Ondrei. Can't you see?"

Tears shone on her lashes when she opened her eyes again. "I am not the woman you need. I'm not a woman at all. This body I wear—it's only a container. I cannot love you. I was given a task, a sacred duty. This nation, though small, will play a mighty part in the history of the world. A day will come, long after you are gone, when this nation will be all that stands between life and death, between good and evil. I cannot tell you the things I have Seen that are to come. I was left as the defender of this nation. If I give in to love, I will lose the part of me that is destined to defend."

"Why can't you have both?" He knew he was begging, but he could not let this chance slip away, not when he was so close to winning her. "Why can't you have love, even if it only lasts a short while in the span of your life, and then continue on after?"

"If I make that choice, I will become fully human. I will die, and there will be no one left to defend Legerdemain from what is to come."

"If you die, then our children will live on, and they will defend us." He leaned down, his lips almost to hers.

"Stop!" She shoved him back with a pulse of magic that sent him thudding on his backside.

"I am not for you," she said, her eyes stony again. "I cannot choose love, but if I could, it wouldn't be you."

She turned and stalked back toward her tent without looking back.

He stared after her. She'd seemed so vulnerable. She wanted love—she'd said as much. But if not him, then who?

Traps

Ada stood at the edge of the battlefield, watching in the dark as the men pulled a cart piled high with chairs and benches in a haphazard stack toward the river. The non-existent weapon was still spelled so that it glowed. It would strike fear into the enemy, but it would be minutes, at best, before they realized it wasn't actually doing anything in the battle. It would give them a few moments of advantage, and then they'd be overwhelmed.

Unless by some miracle Elya managed to convince her uncle that he should just go home.

It was worth a try—everything was worth a try at this point—but Ada had seen his type before. He would not just give up. The lust for power and control overwhelmed him. Legerdemain's refusal to bow before him and be conquered only made him more determined to win. Elya would go to him for one last effort to bluff him out of the war, but it Ada felt certain it wouldn't work. In the morning, Ryshael would attack, and unless a miracle or three materialized, Legerdemain would be wiped out.

"What is it?"

Ada turned at the sound of Cornan's voice. "What is what?"

"You're more nervous than a cat in a barn full of dogs." Cornan reached out to take her hand. "Tell me what you need."

She laughed dryly. "There are so many things I need."

"Are kisses among them?"

Despite her worry, the corners of her lips twitched. She'd hardly spoken to him since he'd seen her with Ondrei in bed. Not that anything had happened. Not that it meant anything. But she'd been worried about what he thought. He'd seemed so angry, so distant that day. But now here he was, teasing and flirting. "Hardly," she smirked.

"Pity. I have those in plentiful supply."

"I'm sure you do. Do you, by any chance, have a miracle hiding up your sleeve?"

"I have the next best thing."

"And what's that?"

"Faith."

"I wish I could say the same."

"Oh, Ada. If you could see what I see. I see a people who hold on to hope despite all odds. I see a king who is trying his very best to be worthy of his role. And I see you. All power and strength and beauty, who will never surrender. We are watching you. All of us. And we will fight because you give us the strength to go on."

"All the strength in the world may not be enough."

"And yet it may."

"Cornan…" she turned to look at him and almost got lost in his eyes. But she needed to say this—needed him to know. "Even if we win, I will not be free. I have a duty. I made a choice a long time ago, and I cannot break the vows I made, as much as I would like to."

Cornan smiled, his eyes sad. "I know. I've always known. I hoped, but I never really thought things would be different. But I made a choice, too. I will follow you to death if need be, and it doesn't matter if nothing can ever come of it—I will always love you."

She let him pull her into his arms. It was unfair of her to let him continue, but right now… right now she needed his strength as much as he needed hers. The morning might witness the death of both of them, but tonight…

She stayed in his embrace until nervousness forced her to pace again.

"Would it help you to have a plan in place? For when they discover that the weapon is fake?"

She nodded, grateful to be doing something, at least. "What kind of plan do you have in mind?"

"They'll be crossing the river, and their first objective will be to destroy the weapon. If it were me, I'd try to set it on fire. Flaming arrows or something. So we need a way to make that backfire on them. When they destroy it, it destroys them."

"Yes. I can do that. I can put a spell on it that will explode and send a wave of… fire, do you think? Would that work?"

111

Cornan nodded. "That would work well. Is there a way to—I don't know, set up flammable things so they catch fire and surround the Ryshaelans after the spell goes off?"

"Yes. Yes, I can do that. Come on."

Ada conscripted a few of the soldiers on duty and made her way to the cart that carried the weapon. In addition to the other spells on it, she laid one that would cause flames to burst out. From there, she had the soldiers use wood and logs to build small pyres in a wide circle, and she connected those with magic to the weapon. When the Ryshaelans set the weapon on fire—and if they didn't, then the Legerdemainians could when the Ryshaelans were close enough—the weapon would explode and send a wave of fire to the other pyres, trapping those close by in a circle of magical fire.

When she was finished, Cornan wrapped an arm around her waist. "How are you feeling about that?"

"Good," she said. "Let's do another one. If we can trap several groups, then we can deal with them one at a time."

"You need to rest. Tomorrow is going to be a long day."

"I can rest when we win. I still have time to set up a few more traps. And by then, Elya should be back with news from the Ryshaelan camp."

"Can some of the other sorcerers help with this?"

"No. It would take too long to teach them the spell. Besides, I want them to be fresh and well-rested in the morning."

"But that doesn't apply to you?"

"I have a different threshold for exhaustion than they do."

"Like Cadalanian wine, you get more appealing the longer I look at you."

"Well, I guess we can worry about that after we win this little battle tomorrow."

Her throat tightened. Even in the midst of what might well be their doom, he still tried to make her smile.

She reached out and squeezed his hand before laying the next spell onto the pyre in the field.

The night was more than halfway past when she finally felt she had set enough of the traps. "Let's get back to the tent," she said. "Elya should be back soon."

Cornan held her hand as they walked in silence, until just before they reached the circle of tents. In a few short hours, everything would change. She had one tiny window in which she could be utterly selfish.

112

She stopped and turned to face him. "Cornan?"

He smiled down at her. "Yes, Ada?"

"I lied before."

"Oh?" His impish grin quirked his lips. "About what?"

"I am thinking about you kissing me."

Cornan's arms slipped around her waist, and before she could take another breath, his lips were on hers, warm and comforting, hard and passionate all at once. She slid her arms around his neck and pulled in closer to him, drinking in the comfort and fervor that he poured out until the thought of war disappeared behind a veil of love.

Sabotage

Elya tried to sleep, but rest wouldn't come. Tonight, she would face her uncle. She'd already betrayed him, and her country, but this was worse. This was more than just reporting his activities and spreading gossip.

Tonight, she would bring trained warriors into her old camp to destroy her former countrymen. Tonight, she went beyond traitor. Tonight she became the enemy incarnate.

After tonight, if she survived, she could not return home. It would be the last night she would see her uncle, the man who had raised her after he'd defeated her father in combat.

Tonight, she went from passively collecting information to actively attacking.

Tonight, she became Legerdemainian.

She'd met the other sorcerers in training, but her mind was too full to remember the names of the three who joined her—two men and a woman.

"This way." She led the way along the path she'd worn through the forest to the bank of the river where her little makeshift bridge still held.

"Is that… safe?" one of the men asked.

"It will hold," she said. "Although you're welcome to make your own if you prefer." She walked across and the others followed, though there was a collective sigh of relief when they were all across.

They followed her silently across the field until she held up her hand for them to stop. "This is where the patrol comes to. I will incapacitate him. That will give you enough time before the next one discovers him to get into the camp. I will need to check in with my uncle, and then I will join you. We will need to work quickly—cut horse lines and tent lines. Last of all, we'll set supply tents and weapons tents on fire, and then we'll need to escape as quickly as possible."

She pointed to one of the men. "Get four horses when you cut the lines and bring them back here. There will be chaos when things start burning, and we don't want them to get spooked. Then meet us back at the supply tents."

"Won't someone try to stop me if they see me leading four horses away?"

"Maybe. Just tell them Lord Broden asked for them, and insist they go ask him if they have a problem with it. Broden is a temperamental dictator, and no one will want to cross him."

The man nodded.

"Best of luck," Elya said.

She strode forward and hailed the patrol as he came toward her.

"I have news," she panted as though she'd been running. "I need to see the king immediately."

He jerked his head toward the camp. "You know which way to go."

She nodded and reached for his hand. "Thank you."

She sent a jolt of magic through him, making his body spasm and slump to the ground. She hoped he hadn't been seriously injured... then resigned herself to the fact that she couldn't afford leniency or mercy. Her uncle and those under his command certainly wouldn't show any.

She ran toward the camp, past the second patrol, on whom she performed the same spell, and dashed for her uncle's tent.

"Majesty, I have news."

Her uncle turned stood from where he sat eating his dinner.

"They're moving the weapon," she blurted out before he could respond further. "They've put it on a cart, and they're hauling it toward the river. Their construction crews are building a ramp bridge as we speak. By morning, it will be across the river. You must disband the army immediately."

Her uncle stepped toward her slowly. She didn't like the look in his eyes. She'd seen that look before.

Her uncle raised his hand and smashed his fist against her face, sending her tumbling to the ground, black spots dotting her vision.

"Did you think I wouldn't find out?" he spat. "That I wouldn't figure out you'd been playing me this whole time?"

"I don't understand," Elya whimpered from her landing place on the floor.

"Broden saw you coming out of the king's tent after his meeting. Saw you talking to their sorceress."

"No, you don't understand. They found out where I was from. I had to go along with it—I needed them to believe I'd defected. I told them only the barest minimum so they would believe I was on their side."

He slammed his fist into her face again, knocking her backwards, her head thunking on the hard ground. "Liar! You've been working against me for a long time, and now I have all the pieces. What did you think would happen when the supply masters said you'd been taking carts across the river that our troops never received? Or when the reports got back to me that you were the one who told people about the weapon?"

A sharp flash of pain jolted through her as he kicked her in the stomach.

She curled up on herself, drawing her knees to her chest, gasping to breathe.

"How long?" He kicked her again. "When did you decide to betray me?" *Kick.* "What have you told them?"

She didn't answer. Even if she wanted to, she couldn't form words against the constant barrage of his feet against her body.

He leaned down and grabbed her by the hair, yanking her up. He backhanded her across the face again. Her mouth filled with blood.

She slumped, but he still held her by the hair, and she fought to regain her footing, to take some of the pressure off her scalp.

He half-dragged her out of the tent.

"Get shackles," he demanded.

One of the guards went running.

Her uncle continued to drag her by her hair until they arrived at a tree in the center of the camp. The guard arrived a moment later, and her uncle clamped one shackle around her wrist, then tossed the chain over a large branch above her head and clamped her other wrist, so she was dangling by her wrists, her feet scarcely brushing the ground. Her whole body hurt, as bruises formed. Every breath came in a spasm of agony and her mind felt so thick she could scarcely thing.

Her uncle paced back and forth in front of her.

"Stupid girl. Did you really think you could win? That by betraying me you would somehow maneuver yourself into a position of power? I. Will. Destroy. You."

Tears stung the cuts on her face. She choked on blood, and her jaw swelled so she could hardly move it.

Her uncle stopped pacing to stare at her. "You joined the enemy. Why? Never mind, it doesn't matter why. You've been sabotaging me ever since. You came tonight to tell me something. Something important enough to risk being caught."

"Majesty!" someone shouted

The king turned and a guard dragged someone along beside him.

The sorcerer—the one Elya had told to get horses.

The sorcerer saw Elya, and even through her swollen eyes, she saw the panic that contorted his features.

A blaze of magical energy formed in his hands, and he launched it at the guard.

The guard toppled, and the sorcerer fell to the ground a moment later, her uncle's knife protruding from his chest.

Her uncle turned to face her. "You brought a sorcerer? Into my camp?"

She didn't answer.

"How many more?" Without waiting for a response, he called out to his guards. "Search the camp. We have intruders. Kill them on sight— they are sorcerers. Don't give them a chance to use magic on you."

He looked at her, stared deep into her eyes, understanding dawning across his face.

"The weapon. You came to tell me they were bringing the weapon across the river. You told me to disband the army and run. But everything out of your mouth is a lie. Which means... there is no weapon."

He stalked away, calling out to his guards as he went. "Ready the troops. We attack at dawn."

Seeing

"She should've been back by now." Ada paced the War Council tent. She'd told Ondrei to get some rest, as she should be doing, but they both still sat, waiting for news.

"She probably just got delayed," Ondrei said.

"And the others?"

"Must be waiting for her. They'll be back soon."

"And if they're not?" Ada stared at him. "What then?"

"Then we proceed as planned. We assemble the army and march toward the river. We bring the cart with the weapon and try to bluff our way through."

"And what happens when they realize that the weapon isn't doing anything? That we have nothing?"

"Then we fight to the death to protect our people."

Ada closed her eyes. Something was wrong. She could feel it.

"Ada, come here."

She turned to look at the king, draped across his chair. She took a wary step toward him.

He reached out and took her hand. She didn't pull back. He needed to feel the comfort of her presence. She needed to continue to be strong for him.

"I love you," he said. Simply, without any agenda. Just a statement.

Ada sighed. "I know."

"We'll get through this. You said yourself there are prophecies that have yet to be fulfilled."

"The prophecies will come true, one way or another. The future cannot be changed. But prophecies rarely come true in the way we think they will. It usually isn't until long afterward that we know how they came about."

"But it's clear the royal line persists, right?"

"I wish I knew, Ondrei. But that was not a vision I Saw. I can't interpret something someone else wrote down."

"But you can See other things. Can you See what will happen tomorrow? What is happening now?"

She nodded. "Perhaps. I will try."

The Healers' tent was still buzzing with activity. The Healers worked in shifts to provide continuing care to the wounded.

"Good evening, my lady," Gerdwin said. "Can I help you?"

"I need to borrow some supplies. I'll just be a moment."

"Of course. What are you going to do?"

"I'm going to try to See. Would you like to learn how?"

"I would, very much, if you have time to teach me."

She gathered the supplies of herbs and a bowl, and led Gerdwin to her own tent, where it was quiet. "You can use other herbs, but just like in Healing, different things will be more effective for some spells than for others. I prefer sage, because it helps clear your mind, chamomile, because it helps bring clarity, and mint, because it sharpens your focus."

She mixed the herbs with water in the bowl and took Gerdwin's hand. "Just a little thread of magic, directed into the water. Seeing is basically opening a window into another place and time. You can See across distances and Time. What is cannot be changed, but what you See isn't always what you think you See. Visions must be weighed and interpreted very carefully to understand the truth."

She opened the window so she could See Elya.

And nearly shattered the magic that let her See.

Elya hung by her wrists from the branch of a tree, her whole body a mass of bleeding wounds and bruises. Around her, the Ryshaelan army moved like ants, scurrying around and readying to move.

But not away—they were not disbanding and going home in fear. They were preparing to attack.

Ada backed away from the bowl. "Go get the king," she said, her voice a hoarse whisper.

Gerdwin stared at the bowl, frozen.

"Go now!"

Gerdwin jumped and ran from the tent.

Ada took a deep breath and stared into the bowl again. She adjusted the window to look in at the Ryshaelan king.

He was preparing his armor. That meant he was coming with his troops, not staying behind as he had before.

Which meant this was the end. The entire Ryshaelan army, not just bits and segments of it, would be crossing the river.

She scanned the Ryshaelan camp. Some of the men were already sawing down trees and lashing logs together to make bridges. She could send a dove to the dam to have them store up water and release it in a wave again, but they would be prepared for that as soon as they saw the river starting to go down. Not to mention that they'd take advantage of the respite to get as many men and horses across as possible before the river struck again.

The flap of her tent swung open and Ondrei burst in.

Cornan was with him.

Her heart tightened at the sight of him. The kiss they'd shared lingered on her lips, begging her to succumb to another. She blinked away the desire.

It didn't matter anyway. She couldn't pursue any line of thought that included him in her life. It could never be.

And yet…

She swallowed that thought, too, and turned away from his deep, compassionate gaze.

"What is it?" Ondrei demanded.

"Look," she said, pointing to the bowl.

Ondrei peered into the water. "I don't understand what I'm Seeing."

"Ryshael is preparing to attack. Somehow they found out about Elya. They know about the weapon. They'll be starting to cross the river within the hour, and they'll be upon us, probably hoping to catch us while most of the army is still asleep."

The blood drained from Ondrei's face. "What do we do?"

"Wake everyone. Especially the sorcerers. They'll be expecting to take us by surprise, so have the sorcerers stationed on the road just as they are coming out of the forest. If we can take them by surprise, it may give us an advantage."

"All the advantage in the world won't help us now," Ondrei said, staring into the bowl at the mass of bodies that began to get into formation. "They're going to destroy us."

Ada walked over to him and slapped his face. "Do not say things like that. Ever. I was given the responsibility to take care of this land, and I will defend it to my dying breath—and as you know, I am very hard to kill. That includes defending it from your defeatist attitudes."

Ondrei stared at her as though seeing her for the first time.

She sighed and placed a gentle hand on his cheek where she'd slapped him. "These people need you. They need to see you in all your power. Remember what I taught you. This is the hour in which you must be the leader that you were born to be. I will do what I can, but you need to show these people who you truly are. Why you were chosen to be king of this country. The blood that runs in your veins is more powerful than you can imagine. Embrace it. Be the king—be the *sorcerer*—that we need."

For the first time in his life, Ada saw in his eyes the gleam of strength and determination that had passed to him from his ancestors. The spark of magic that flowed through him.

She smiled.

They hadn't lost this war yet.

Prisoner

Pain burned into Elya's wrists as she dangled. Her breath came in short, stifled gasps as she struggled to lift herself on her toes far enough to suck in the air. Bruises covered every part of her body, and blood trickled down from the shackles around her wrists.

All around her, the noise of preparations being made created a din, but she could scarcely hear it over the pounding in her ears.

What would happen when they left to invade Legerdemain? Would her uncle leave her here to die? Would he take her with them? Send her with a contingent of soldiers back to the capital?

No, it wouldn't be that. He didn't care enough for her to waste any of his soldiers taking her back. He would use every man in the battle. Every man he had left, anyway. About a third had defected and run away after she'd planted rumors.

That, at least, was a small victory.

But it wasn't enough. It was never enough. Her uncle knew there was no weapon. The one tactic they'd had to stall him, and now it was gone. And it was her fault. She'd gotten too cocky, too sure of herself and her ability to lie and play both sides. She'd failed Legerdemain. Failed Ada, who was only trying to protect her people.

Failed Ondrei.

When had she started thinking of him as just "Ondrei" and not "His Majesty"? She didn't know. But suddenly her failure to help him seemed worse than all her other failures.

What would he think of her when he woke in the morning to a full-scale invasion? He would believe she'd betrayed him. He would think the worst of her.

That thought hurt more than the lashes on her back or the iron digging into her wrists.

Perhaps, if he survived, he'd find her body, and he'd know she'd died faithful to him.

To him? What was she thinking? The pain and loss of blood must be making her delirious. She wasn't his. She'd chosen Legerdemain, but he was the king. He didn't care for her more than for any of the other sorcerers.

And in the morning, he would be overwhelmed. Her uncle would not let him live. He would be hunted down, and he would die thinking she'd betrayed him.

She couldn't let that happen. She had to warn him somehow.

But she could barely move, barely think. She couldn't escape.

And yet she would. She had to.

She opened her eyes, as far as she could against the swelling around them. "Help me." Her voice came out in a hoarse croak.

She swallowed to force some moisture into her mouth and tried again. "Help me!"

One of the stable hands paused in his scurrying to look at her.

"Water," she begged.

He looked around, as though to see if he would be punished for helping her, then trotted to one of the cisterns and filled up a ladle. He put it to her lips and she sucked down the cool water, soothing her parched throat.

"Thank you," she whispered. "One more? Please?"

The boy nodded and returned a moment later with another ladleful.

He paused when she was done and looked around again, but no one paid them any attention.

"Did you..." He paused before going on. "Did you really betray your own uncle?"

She was probably going to die anyway. She might as well make it count. "Yes. My uncle is an evil man. Legerdemain is filled with good, honest people who only want to be left alone. He will destroy them for his own power, and take their country. He will slaughter everyone, for no other reason than his own ambition."

"But... they practice magic," the boy said, as though that fact alone made everything right.

Elya slowly moved her head up and down. "Yes. But magic isn't bad. That's a lie, told by my uncle in order to keep his people under control. Magic is useful and... beautiful."

The boy's eyes widened but he didn't run away from her supposed blasphemy.

"My father… he's a soldier. He was wounded in the last skirmish. He said he was struck by magic."

Elya nodded. "Yes. They are outnumbered ten to one. If ten men were coming to kill you and steal everything you loved, wouldn't you use whatever tools you had to protect yourself?"

The boy blinked, weighing her words.

"Please—I can barely breathe. Will you get me a block of wood to stand on?"

The boy nodded and hurried back with a log from the fire. It wobbled, but it was enough for her to get some leverage so she could breathe.

"I… I should get back to work."

"Thank you. For the water, and for the log." Now that she could breathe, an idea began to form in her mind. "What is your name?"

"Londen," the boy replied.

"Londen, where is your father?"

"In the infirmary tent."

"And his name?"

"Rendon."

"Is the infirmary tent staying here while the army crosses the river?"

"I think so, my lady."

"When I escape, I will help your father. Remember that it was I, Elya, who helped him when King Jando left him to die."

The boy's eyes bugged nearly out of his face, but he nodded before turning to run back toward the horses.

Elya breathed deeply, filling her lungs with air. She couldn't believe she hadn't thought of it before. The only explanation was that her mind was too muddled with pain to focus. But now…

She closed her eyes and focused on the magic all around. It was rich here, untapped. Flowing freely all around those who would deny its existence.

She pulled the magic into herself, into her wounds. The energy soothed the aches and knit together her broken skin. It would be better if someone else Healed her, but it was enough to give her a reprieve.

When the pain had dulled enough for her to move, she wove a thread of magic into the lock that clamped her shackles.

The lock clicked open.

She stood for a moment, just holding the shackles in her hands, and looked around. Most of the activity had moved away from this part of the camp as the army prepared to cross the river.

She waited another moment to make sure no one was watching, then released the shackles and scurried behind the tree.

One quick burst at a time, from tree to bush to empty tent, she made her way to the back of the camp where the infirmary tent sat.

The stench of infection and decay filled her nostrils before she even got close. Was anyone even in there tending to the wounded? Or had her uncle just left them alone to die slowly?

She crept quietly to the door of the tent, stifling the urge to retch. The moans and ragged breathing of the men inside floated out. She listened for the sound of anyone moving around, footsteps that would indicate a physician, but there was nothing.

Her uncle had left them to die. But she would help them live.

The Amulet

Ondrei stood at the front of his troops on the battlefield. Darkness still shrouded the sky. The moon had set and the stars sent pricks of light smattering across the sky. He looked up at the Hunter, his bow outstretched as he took aim at the Hart.

Normally, that would be a good omen. A sign that he would be victorious in the hunt.

But was he the Hunter or the Hart?

The amethyst amulet hanging around his neck glowed against his chest. Was that an omen, too? And if so, was it good or bad?

Ada rode up beside him. Her face held its usual expressionless serenity, but her hands clenched her horse's reins and her breathing was shallow.

What wouldn't he give to be the one to soothe and comfort her!

He exhaled slowly. That would never happen. He could woo and wish until his deathbed, but Ada was not one to relent. And she was right, of course. She always was. If they survived this battle, he would have to seek elsewhere for love.

"What news on Elya?" he asked.

"Nothing new. Last I Saw, she was still hanging from the tree."

"When we win, we'll go rescue her."

"When we win." Ada smiled, but her jaw was tight. "Ondrei, there's something you must know. Something I've been trying to show you gradually, but now, we have no more time. I need to tell you about the Amulet."

He looked down again at the amethyst. "You told me it was passed down from the first king of Legerdemain and that gemstones are useful for enhancing magical energy."

126

"Yes. But there's more. That is no ordinary gemstone. It is a sacrifice."

"What do you mean?"

"When humans first came to this land, it was inhabited by dragons. They formed an alliance, a treaty for all of time. The dragons knew their time among men was coming to an end, so they imbued some of their magic to the humans. The First King was given this amulet as a gift."

She lifted the gemstone on its chain. "Look around the edges, at the words inscribed. Those words are the last line of a prophecy. A promise, if you will, of the end of this age. And the amethyst itself is more than an ordinary gem, more than a simple conduit. It is imbued with magic, forged in dragon fire, and connected by blood to the First King."

Ondrei traced the letters. "What does that mean?"

"It means you are part of a greater whole. The gemstone could be used by another, in theory, but the magic that resides therein is intimately connected to you and to your blood. You can wield it. If you let it, it will be the most powerful weapon in the world. Dragon magic is some of the most powerful in existence, and it was entrusted to the First King, to be used to protect this land until the dragons return."

She lifted her hand and touched his cheek. "You have been given a sacred duty to protect this land, much as I have. You are connected to it. If you die, this land dies, and with it, the future. I was given the duty to protect you, and your ancestors before you and your children after you, but *you* were given this nation."

She pulled her hand away and waved it toward the south. "They are coming because they believe the weapon does not exist. They believe they know a secret—that our magic is impotent and that they can overwhelm us. But they are wrong. *You* are the weapon. You are more powerful than even the worst images we planted in the minds of the Ryshaelan spies. Surrender to the magic within you, and you can defeat your enemy and protect your people."

Ondrei inhaled, letting the cold morning air sear through him. The amulet seemed to burn in his hand, though it didn't cause any pain.

He had a duty, to his people, to his country. He would not let them be overwhelmed by Ryshael. He would not let them be destroyed. He would not let the land die.

Closing his eyes, he felt the magic in the amulet. It shone more brilliantly than the shafts of lightning that Ada produced or the glow that he'd used to enhance his sword. He relaxed into it, and let it fill him, the way he'd done with other magic from the air.

This was... he couldn't even describe the sensation. He felt like he was glowing from the inside out, shining like a star. He was one with the amulet itself. He could feel the breath of an ancient dragon breathing life into him, could feel the magic of the ancient beings infusing him with strength.

The strength that could build—or rebuild a kingdom. The strength that could save lives.

The same strength that would incinerate the greedy, power-hungry dictator who sought to destroy them.

He opened his eyes. Despite the pre-dawn darkness, he could see clearly. He could see the trees in the forest, and the glimpses of the river beyond through the gap where the road went. And he could feel the land pulsing beneath him.

On the battlefield stood an army. A beautiful woman with dark hair and titled eyes, her hands glowing with magic.

Elya.

His magical mirage, through which untold power would lash out at his enemy.

This land was his, and after today, no one would try to take it again. They would learn it could not be done by force.

Ada smiled at him. "There you are. The king I knew you could be. Come, Your Majesty. Let us defend this land. I will be by your side through the entire battle, protecting you."

From behind them, a soldier rode up to position himself next to Ada.

"And I'll be protecting you," he said.

Ada smiled at the soldier, a look in her eyes that Ondrei had dreamed of her casting his way. He stifled a sigh. So that was the way of it. But somehow, he didn't mind as much. Perhaps it was the magic filling him to overflowing with love for his country. Perhaps he was just growing wiser. Whatever the case, he did not resent her—or the soldier—for their choice.

His first love was Legerdemain.

Today, he would protect *her*, and as for a woman to share his life... well, he could think about a second love tomorrow.

Healer

Elya slipped inside the infirmary tent and knelt next to the man closest to the entrance. He was still breathing. She placed a hand on his chest and sent a tendril of magic into him to determine what ailed him.

His whole left side was damaged. His left leg was dead—there was nothing to be done for it—and his arm was nearly so. A wound in his left side festered. She drew on the magic and pushed it into him. First, his leg, sealing off the arteries from the infection lower down, and healing the bottom part. The dead portion would fall off—she could feel it, even now, beginning to detach. Next, his arm. She used the magic to get the blood flowing freely to his fingertips so his arm would not die as his leg had. Finally, the wound in his side. She killed the infection and knit the flesh back together.

By the time she was finished, she could hardly move. It had expended a tremendous amount of energy to make the trees grow, but this…

The man stirred and she put a hand on his forehead. "What is your name?" she asked.

"Soro," he mumbled.

"Sh, Soro." she whispered. "Rest now. You will lose your leg, but you will live. And when you wake, remember that when Jando left you to die, Elya saved you."

She ran a faint trickle of magic into his mind to help him rest, then moved on to the next man. She could not do such extensive healing on all of them. It would drain her of strength she needed to get back to help Legerdemain.

But she could help.

One by one, she touched each of the wounded, healing the wounds that were life-threatening and killing infections so they could heal on their own. She told each one the same thing—to remember when he woke that Jando had left him to die and Elya had saved him. She asked each man his name, but did not find Londen's father, Rendon, even after Healing everyone in the tent.

Was there another infirmary tent? Or was Rendon already dead?

She slipped out of the tent and breathed deeply of the fresh air. Despite her Healing, the infirmary tent still stank of death.

She walked around to the back side. There, lying on the ground, was a man in a physician's uniform, a bottle in his hand.

She nudged him.

He drooled a little and sat up. "What… what is it?"

"You're the physician?" she asked.

He glanced up and down at her, his eyes lingering on the shreds of her dress where the whip had torn but where the flesh was now healing. "You injured?"

Rage filled her at the sight of the physician in a drunken stupor when he should've been helping. "Why are you out here when your charges are dying inside?"

"There's nothing I can do for them. They're too far gone, and I… I couldn't take the smell anymore."

She clenched her jaw. She'd deal with him later.

"I'm looking for a man named Rendon. He was injured in the battle. Where is he? Is he dead?"

The physician shook his head. "Naw, he was one o' the ones wasn't so bad. He's in that tent over there, with those what might make it, not with these that will waste away in a few days."

"Thank you. But don't be so sure about the men in this tent. Check on them in the morning."

She hurried toward the other tent, leaving the physician gaping at her.

"Rendon?" she whispered once she was inside. Then again, a little louder, "Rendon?"

A grunt came from one of the mats, and she hurried over. She touched his arm and he sat up.

"Are you Rendon?"

"I am. Who are you?"

"I am Elya. The king's niece."

"Why are you here?"

131

Elya placed her hands on his arm and sent magic through him. His leg was broken, but it would heal on its own, in time, and there was a slash along his arm where magical lighting had struck him. The heat had cauterized the wound, but it was still tender and healing, and in danger of infection.

"Your son saved my life. This is to thank him for his service." She sent the magic deep into him, fully healing his leg and arm.

"Remember me," she said. "When the king is no more, I will be your queen."

She checked the others in the tent for infection, Healing those who needed it, then hurried out of the tent.

The faintest gray light tinged the sky to the east. The camp was mostly quiet now. The army had begun its journey to the river. If she hurried, maybe she could still warn Ondrei.

Or at least let him know that she hadn't betrayed him.

She ran toward one of the supply tents. A guard was stationed there, lolling against the post that held the tent erect.

She shot a blast of magic at him, sending him crumpling to the ground. After stripping him to his underclothes, she dressed in his uniform and grabbed his sword, then took some dried meat and fruit from the tent.

One lone horse stood in the corral, favoring one foot.

It wasn't broken, or they would've killed the animal, but it was no good for charging into battle.

Elya placed her hands on the horse's neck and Healed it.

The horse nickered, thanking her by nuzzling her with its nose. "There's a good fellow. Are you all right to let me ride you?"

He snorted and tossed his head.

Elya saddled and mounted him and turned him toward the east.

Dawn crept over the horizon. In the distance, the sounds of battle had already begun to fill the air.

"My lady," a voice called out.

Elya turned her horse and her heart stuttered at the sight before her. A whole contingent of men stood behind her carrying swords.

Were they going to try to stop her? To kill her?

She started to turn, intending to flee.

"My lady, wait." It was a boy's voice.

She turned.

Londen.

"Are you going to fight the king?" the boy asked.

Elya nodded. "Yes."

"We want to help."

Elya looked out over the sea of men who had begun to gather.

"It's true, my lady," a man said. "We defected from the army. We've been in hiding in the hills to the south, waiting to see how the war would turn out and if we could return home or if we would need to leave for good. The lad told us about you. We want to follow you instead of your uncle."

Elya grinned. "Very well, then. Come on."

War

Ondrei could see, through his magically enhanced vision, the shock on the faces of the enemy as they swarmed the battlefield in the pre-dawn light to find that they had not taken Legerdemain by surprise.

They'd forded the river and pushed through the trees, and now spread out along the field.

There was a moment of confusion as the soldiers paused, waiting for direction. They'd hoped to slaughter the Legerdemainian army as they slept, to overcome them while they scrambled to heed the warnings of whatever lookouts would be on duty. Seeing the Legerdemainian army, complete with sorcerers whose hands blazed with magic, standing ready, made them pause. Then their eyes adjusted to not only the sight of the army, ready and waiting, but the hundreds of representations of Elya, the spy who'd defected, wielding magic against them.

The vision sent a palpable wave of bewilderment and fear through the Ryshaelans.

A man with Elya's olive skin and tilted eyes rode at the center of the swarm. Could he be Elya's uncle? The king? Jando?

Jando raised his sword arm. "It's more of their sorcery! She isn't real! Attack!" His signal sent a contingent toward the cart that carried the false weapon. He sent another contingent the other direction, to flank the eastern side of the Legerdemanian army.

Straight toward another of Ada's traps.

Per Ada's advice, Legerdemain would wait before entering the fray. This would throw Ryshael off-balance. First, because they wouldn't know why Legerdemain wasn't attacking, and second, because when they tried to destroy the weapon they would receive plenty of damage themselves, which would send panic through them, wondering if the weapon was real after all. Then the other traps would isolate groups of them, making them easier to dispatch.

Ondrei glanced at Ada and she gave him a slight nod and a smile, indicating that the plan was still in place.

They waited.

The first group of Ryshaelans drew near enough to the weapon to attack the guards surrounding it. The guards had instructions to make a show of defending the weapon, then fall back outside the line that would be created with magical fire.

As Cornan had predicted, the Ryshaelans were going to use fire. One of them had a small pot which presumably contained coals, because when they threw tinder into it, the pale glow of fire began to form.

At the first sign of flames, the Legerdemainian guards retreated.

Jando noticed and began waving his arms, clearly not trusting what was about to happen.

But it was too late.

The archers lit their pitch-tipped bows from the flaming pot and, as one, fired upon the weapon.

Blue and gold flames erupted from the cart, sending Ryshaelan bodies flying backward. An instant later, the flames lanced out, igniting the small bonfires that encircled the weapon, trapping at least a hundred Ryshaelans inside the ring of magical flame.

As predicted, chaos ensued amongst the Ryshaelans. Some tried to go back the way they had come, only to be trampled by their cohorts.

Jando pressed forward, urging his army to continue the surge.

When they were within range, Ada gave the order to ignite the other traps.

Half a dozen magical flame circles leapt up, each trapping a crowd of Ryshaelans in fire that they could not get through. The fire would burn itself out within an hour, Ada had said, but in the meantime, would incinerate anyone who tried to pass through it.

Still, Ryshael pushed forward.

Ondrei looked at Ada.

She nodded, her face solemn. "It's time," she said.

Ondrei raised his sword and let the magic from the amulet flow through him, filling him with power and making his sword glow.

His army charged to meet Ryshael's.

Ada rode just in front of him, to keep any of the Ryshaelans from getting to him, and Cornan rode in front of her to do the same. He saw again the way Cornan looked at Ada and felt a pang of regret. Not that he blamed the man. Who could resist falling for her?

But he also saw the way she looked at him, and wondered if her choice to deny herself love would extend even after the war.

He quickly pushed those thoughts aside, however, as the armies clashed against one another.

Lighting and other magical bursts leaped from the hands of the sorcerers, including the army of Elyas, slicing through the Ryshaelans. Swords and spears from both sides clanged and struck, and the moans of the dying soon filled the air.

Ada pulled back until she was beside him and took his hand. The warmth of Healing and strength flowed from her into him. "It's time, Ondrei. Protect your people."

Ondrei closed his eyes and pulled as much magic into himself as he could bear, then sent it out again, a concussive pulse that made the earth roll beneath the feet of the Ryshaelan army in one long wave. Men and horses launched into the air and then fell crashing to the ground. Some got up and pressed forward, only to fall again when Ondrei sent the next pulse.

His stomach churned. Killing with magic went against everything he wanted to be as a king—as a man.

But the hope that lit the eyes of his army as they advanced on those who survived filled him with renewed purpose.

The Ryshaelans began to reform, moving sideways, out of the path of the earthquakes Ondrei directed into them.

Taking a deep breath, he focused on a spot just to the east, where a huge group of Ryshaelans was making their way toward the eastern flank of the Legerdemainian army.

He felt the earth, the plants, the air—and ripped them apart. A fissure formed as the earth cracked, a giant hole that swallowed hundreds of Ryshaelans before Ondrei could no longer hold it open.

His strength waned and he dropped his arms.

In an instant, Ada was at his side, pouring magical renewal into him. Still, it was not enough. It would help for the next attack, but even with the amulet, he could only last a little longer, and still the Ryshaelans swarmed like locusts.

"Just a little more, Ondrei," Ada said. "We can win this. One more spell. You can call upon more lightning than the rest of us combined."

Ondrei nodded. He closed his eyes again and summoned the lightning.

It flashed from the sky, attaching itself to men's swords, charring them from the inside out.

So many dead. So many of his own, too. And yet still they fought. Still they believed in him to save them.

One more attack. One more burst of lightning from a blue sky.

He slumped in his saddle. Even Ada's restorative magic didn't give him enough strength to go on.

He needed one more miracle.

Beside him, Ada gasped.

Ondrei straightened, and looked to where Ada pointed.

Coming through the trees rode a huge contingent of soldiers. They were Ryshaelan, but they weren't attacking Legerdemain—they were attacking the Ryshaelan army from behind.

In their midst, a flash of fire erupted, and a giant fireball landed in the center of a cluster of Ryshaelans.

Ondrei looked again at the figure who led the new contingent.

A woman as beautiful and fierce as Ada raised her hand and sent another fireball into the Ryshaelan army.

Elya had come to save them.

Peace

Ada grinned. She hadn't had time to See if Elya had survived. She'd hoped so. But she'd never expected this. Again, chaos erupted within the Ryshaelan ranks, as the force attacked from behind.

Elya pushed through the crowd, using fireballs—where had she learned how to do that?—to disperse the crowd in front of her as she made her way straight toward Jando.

When she was close, she bent the air, much the same way Ada had done to speak to the Ryshaelans during the first skirmish.

"Stop!" Elya's voice rang out above the din of battle.

The clamoring stopped and all eyes, Ryshaelan and Legerdemainian alike, turned to see her.

She dismounted and stood before her uncle. "As a Daughter of Ryshael, child of a king, and warrior in combat, I hereby challenge you for the throne of Ryshael."

"We are in the middle of a war, you stupid child," Jando said, his voice catching in the spell Elya had cast and carrying over the crowd. "We've almost won. Shut up, or this time I'll kill you."

"There are no laws about when a challenge may be issued. It is my right to challenge you for the throne."

Ada drew closer. It seemed Jando had not yet realized she was using magic.

"You think the Legerdemainians will just stop fighting so they can sit back and watch us duel?"

"They already have," Elya said, nodding toward the Legerdemainian army.

Ada glanced at Ondrei. The smile on his face was much like the one he'd used when looking at her so many times. Good. Elya would be good for him. And he was safe, for the moment. She urged her horse toward the front lines.

"Let me borrow your sword," she said softly to one of the soldiers standing close by where Elya and Jando stared one another down.

The soldier handed it to her, and she poured magic into it, making it blaze with power, its edges sharpened and lengthened, hot to the touch.

Jando lunged, thrusting his sword at Elya. "I killed your father, and I'll kill you, and then I'll kill every man, woman, and child in this cursed land!"

Elya formed a shield of light in her hand and deflected his blow.

His eyes widened as he realized she was a sorceress, but that only served to anger him further. He slashed at her, fury in his eyes. She stepped back, dodging, forming a spell in her hand. She thrust a ball of light at him, sending him stumbling back, but he recovered quickly.

"Elya!" Ada called out.

She tossed the sword, which Elya grabbed from the air and swung. The magic-enhanced blade sliced cleanly through Jando's sword. He used the stub to deflect, but Elya pressed the advantage, sending him tumbling onto his back.

She held the sword above his throat.

"I concede!" he yelled, his voice still echoing through the spell.

"Bind him," Elya said. She turned to face her people. "By right of my lineage and the laws of trial by combat, I am now your queen. I declare this war on Legerdemain ended."

Ondrei rode up next to Ada.

Elya saw him and bowed. "Your Majesty, will you accept our unconditional surrender?"

Jando screamed at her, but was quickly silenced by a sword hilt to his abdomen.

"Your Majesty," Ondrei said, "we have no wish to be at war with your people. If you will leave peacefully, we will not pursue you. Ryshael does not have to be our enemy."

Elya nodded and turned once more to her people. "You heard him. Leave peacefully. If you wish to fight, you will be fighting me, as well."

Those who had followed her across the river hoisted their swords and took on battle stances.

The remaining soldiers looked confused for several long moments, as though weighing the options.

Elya moved to stand by a man who had followed her. "This is the new captain of my guard. His name is Rendon. He will be in the royal tent awaiting my orders. You may make camp and wait for me, or defect to another land, and you will not be pursued. I will return when I have negotiated peace with Legerdemain."

The man she'd called Rendon led the way toward the river, followed first by those who had come with her, and then, slowly, the others followed.

"You will have a long fight ahead of you to maintain control of your people," Ada warned.

"Perhaps. But I have some thoughts I'd like to discuss with you and His Majesty," Elya said.

Ondrei offered Elya his arm. "Let us adjourn to the tavern in the South Village. We have much to discuss."

Ada turned to look for Cornan, but didn't see him. He wasn't among the wounded, so she put him out of her mind and focused on directing the soldiers to form a perimeter and a watch, in case any ambitious Ryshaelans chose to ignore their new queen's orders, and organizing the Healers to tend to the wounded of both armies.

Late that evening, Ada, Ondrei, Elya, and a few surviving members of the War Council sat around the table at the tavern.

"I suppose you'll be wanting to go home now, to tend to your people," Ondrei said to Elya, the note of wistfulness in his voice apparent to Ada.

"This is my home," Elya said. "I've put myself in rather an awkward position, declaring myself queen of a country I have no wish to rule. I do not wish to abandon them, and yet neither do I wish to be part of them. I made my choice when I defected to Legerdemain, and I don't wish to go back. But if I don't, some other cousin or ambitious general will declare his right to rule, and in a few years, we'll be back in this same position."

"Why not give Ryshael the choice to become a vassal state?" one of the War Council generals suggested.

Elya's brow creased in a slight frown. "Ryshael is a blight. Our entire history is one of corruption and a quest for domination. There is no understanding of peace. It is not a nation that should continue to exist. Your Majesty," she turned to Ondrei, "if I may suggest a proposal?"

Ondrei nodded. "I would like to stay here. I would like for my people to have a haven, if they so wish it, so if it is acceptable to you, I

140

will extend the offer to anyone who wishes, to become Legerdemainian. Our land I will sell to Cadalania or Kirland or Sunnland, or bits to each, with the understanding that those who own land retain their rights, but will be answerable to whichever kingdom absorbs that land. And I will disband Ryshael. The country will be no more. I will divide the profit amongst my people who remain, and let them live where they choose."

Admiration shone in Ondrei's eyes. "It's a pity. You would make a wonderful queen."

Elya smiled at him, a hint of flirtation in her eyes. "Perhaps. But only if I had the right kingdom to rule." She stood. "We can discuss the details further in the morning. In the meantime, I need to get some air."

Ada waited until she was gone to speak to Ondrei and the Council. "What do you think?"

"I think there is a lot of work to be done to make sure her people are cared for, but I will accept her surrender," Ondrei said.

The council agreed. And if she were honest, so did Ada. Ryshael was a war-mongering people, and they would be better off scattered to the winds.

That settled, Ada got up.

There was one more thing she had to do.

She walked outside and made her way silently to the town's storm cellar, where Ondrei had imprisoned Jando.

The guard on duty lay sprawled on his back, unconscious.

Ada's heartrate quickened and she hurried down the stone steps.

"I showed you mercy because all the people were watching." Elya's voice.

Ada stopped to listen.

"But if I let you live, there will be those who will try to rescue you, and if they succeed, you will only try again. I can't that happen. Good bye, Uncle."

There was a flash of light, and then silence.

Elya turned to see Ada standing on the foot of the steps. She lifted her chin. "Arrest me if you must."

Ada shook her head. "No, child. I was coming to do the same thing. I will Heal the guard and inform him that Jando died of his injuries. You would do well to be far away when that happens."

"Thank you," Elya said.

Ada nodded and started to walk up the stairs.

"Ada," Elya said.

141

Ada stopped.

"I have a message for you. A man named Cornan asked me to tell you that he went into the mountains to search for buried treasure. But he said, if he succeeds, he will see you again, and he will keep his promises."

Elya trotted up the steps and disappeared into the darkness, but Ada stayed for a long time, trying to figure out what Cornan could have meant.

Buried treasure? What did he mean? And was there a possibility that he would return one day, when she could be free to love him?

Dear Reader,

Thank you for reading **The Sorceress**. This story began as a collection of short stories that I published on the blog I used to write for, New Authors Fellowship (newauthors.wordpress.com). I had no idea when I first wrote *Rendezvous,* the first story in *The Heir*, that I would grow to love this world so much and that the story would grow into what it is today.

I am so excited to finish the stories in *The Amulet Saga*. I hope you'll join me for the rest of the journey.

If you enjoyed this story, please tell a friend. Better yet, buy them their own copy.
You can also purchase The Heir, and The Defector, The Silver Shores, and The Prophecy on Amazon.
Please also check out my first full-length novel, a supernatural thriller called The Breeding!

I love connecting with readers. Please find me on Twitter (@avilyjerome), Instagram (@avilyjeromebooks), my website (www.avilyjerome.com), and Facebook (https://www.facebook.com/AvilyJ?fref=ts).

Yours truly,

Avily Jerome

About the Author

 Avily Jerome is a writer and freelance editor. She spent five years as the Editor of Havok Magazine. Her short stories have been published in multiple magazines, both print and digital. She has judged several writing contests, both for short stories and novels, and she is a book reviewer for Lorehaven Magazine.

She loves all things SpecFic and writes across multiple genres. She is also a writing conference teacher and presenter, and she enjoys speaking to local writers' groups and going to SFF cons.

She is a wife and the mom of five kids. She loves living in the desert in Phoenix, AZ, and when she's not writing, she loves reading, spending time with friends, and experimenting with different art forms.

You can find her on her social media and on her website, at www.avilyjerome.com

www.ingramcontent.com/pod-product-compliance
Lightning Source LLC
Chambersburg PA
CBHW071924220626
47052CB00002B/447